An Angel's
Touch

An Angel's
Touch

HEATHER GRAHAM

KENSINGTON BOOKS
http://www.kensingtonbooks.com

KENSINGTON BOOKS are published by
Kensington Publishing Corp.
119 West 40th Street
New York, NY 10018

All Kensington titles, imprints, and distributed lines are available at special quantity discounts for bulk purchases for sales promotion, premiums,
fund-raising, educational, or institutional use. Special book excerpts or
customized printings can also be created to fit specific needs. For de-
tails, write or phone the office of the Kensington Special Sales Manager:
Attn. Special Sales Department. Kensington Publishing Corp, 119 West
40th Street, New York, NY 10018. Phone: 1-800-221-2647.

Library of Congress Card Catalogue Number: 95-078007

Kensington and the K logo Reg. U.S. Pat. & TM Off.

ISBN-13: 978-1-4967-0867-0
ISBN-10: 1-4967-0867-9
First Kensington Hardcover Edition: November 1995

10 9 8 7 6 5 4 3 2

Printed in the United States of America

PROLOGUE
CHRISTMAS EVE

Fifth Avenue was thronged. Not just ordinary-Fifth-Avenue-thronged, but Christmas-Eve-Fifth-Avenue-thronged. Every few steps, a Salvation Army Santa waved a silver bell; New Yorkers moved at speeded-up paces, even for New Yorkers. They moved in the hundreds, the thousands; throughout the city, they moved in the millions. As Don Angel drove down the street at a snail's pace, looking for his wife, he was convinced that most of Manhattan's population was now on the very street where he searched for Cathy. He squinted against the multitude of bright red and green lights, lights reflecting on the tinsel that decorated store windows, on holly and mistletoe, on Christmas trees, Nativity scenes, garish decorations, frost sprayed on windows, cartoon creatures in Santa hats.

Horns beeped and blared. No true Christmas spirit on the streets of New York! he thought. A taxi screeched in front of him, trying to fit into the foot of space between his car and the old yellow Jaguar ahead of him. A pedestrian, a man exiting the taxi, slammed his fist against the hood of Don's modest gray Beamer.

"Hey!" Don yelled out indignantly. The pedestrian was already on his way, swearing as he dropped a handful of coins into a red Salvation Army pot as he reached the sidewalk.

Christmas. Don shook his head. It was supposed to be a time of good cheer. Good will toward all. Families were supposed to get together. You were just supposed to plain feel good, warm, close to those you loved— happy as all hell. Instead it seemed these days that it all turned into a mania, a shopping frenzy, a fest of greed, hurry—and raging traffic.

He hated Christmas, he decided.

And he could just kill Cathy, he thought, aggravated at being stuck in traffic while wondering if he was going to be able to find her before being forced by the flow into the Christmas-Eve torture of circling the block again. They could have been out of the city by noon; actually, they'd both been at their jobs so long they could easily have taken the day off. Avoided all this rush. But Cathy—Madame Noel—hadn't gotten just the right gift for their niece, little three-year-old Tatiana—Tatiana, a hell of a name for a three-year-old, but then, as Cathy had said, how do you get to be a grown-up Tatiana if you weren't a Tatiana-baby? Cathy had wanted to spend this last afternoon shopping in the city just in case she had forgotten to get a present for anyone else. So, now this.

Not that his day had gone well to begin with. He'd have been better off if he'd stayed home. Actually, he'd have been better off if he'd gone back to grad school and chosen something other than law for his life's work, he thought. He'd graduated damned near the top of his class and taken a job with MacMillan, MacDougal, and MacDouglas, one of the most prestigious firms in what he had considered one of the most important cities on the earth—New York. It was also one of the largest. It seemed to Don that even now, ten years since he had joined the firm—and loyally stayed with them through thick and thin—their promising young attorneys—all right, he was *youngish* at this point—were as plentiful to the powers that be as sheets of toilet paper. And as disposable. He'd half-killed himself over the prep work for the Gerring case, working a good sixty-something-hour week just before the holidays only to have old-Scroogebucket MacMillan decide—at the last minute—this morning that he'd take it over himself.

Bah, humbug. In the nth degree. If he'd just been out of the city, at least he wouldn't have known that Mac-Millan had decided to take the case himself. And maybe it wouldn't have happened. Don was thirty-six, not at all green. But MacMillan was nearly seventy, spry as a nasty warthog, and anyone under fifty was nothing but a pup to him. In truth, Don was certain that MacMillan had taken a good look at him just that morning and determined he was too young to take on such a case. Don shook his head with disgust, thinking of the cases F. Lee Bailey had taken on as a very young man.

Cathy! There she was! Between the girl in the reindeer tights and the old fat lady in the mink coat. Whoa, the fat lady was making mean time, elbowing those in her way out of it almost as if the pedestrians around her were bowling pins. Yep, she shoved Cathy right out of the way.

And Cathy reacted in typical Cathy fashion.

Even as he sighed in frustration, watching her, he felt a twinge of both love and pain stir within him. His wife was a beautiful woman. She'd been blessed with nearly perfect skin, ivory in tone and soft as silk. Her hair was as dark as human hair could be, very sleek; and she wore it in soft waves that just curled around her shoulders. Her eyes were a dark blue, her facial structure was delicate and very classical—she could probably be substituted for a dozen Greek sculptures at the Met. It was her coloring, however, that was so striking, though perhaps even that was enhanced by what was *inside* Cathy. He didn't think he'd ever known someone so alive, so vibrant—and so goddamned Mary Poppinsish. Cathy saw no evil. She never lost patience.

And as the heavyset snowplow of a woman nearly knocked her over, Cathy merely looked surprised, regained her balance, laughed with another woman at her side being jostled leaving the Warner Brothers store, and—he was certain—called out "Merry Christmas" to everyone around her.

She looked up then and saw him trying to ease the Beamer closer to the sidewalk. She waved, that beautiful, eternally cheerful smile curved into her lips, and started hurrying toward the car.

Just as he had nearly achieved the curb to scoop up his wife, one of New York's finest, a mounted policeman he hadn't noticed, rode his horse up to the passenger window.

"No stopping here!" the cop yelled out.

"I'm just—" Don began.

"No stopping! It's guys like you cause this crush— we're going to have gridlock in a minute. Move it!"

"My wife is right—"

"Two seconds and I write you up as a moving violation," the cop said. He slammed a hand down on the top of the Beamer. The mounted cop's horse suddenly snorted all over the Beamer's front passenger window.

Cathy was almost there. Anxiously looking into his eyes. No choice. He hit the gas pedal irritably and jerked forward, forced to turn the corner. She tried to keep up with him, running.

Naturally, the stalled traffic suddenly moved. He started around the block, indicating that he'd get her the next time around. He gritted his teeth hard. At worst, two times around ought to do it. He glanced at his watch. At this rate, they'd make her folks' home in Connecticut just in time to go to sleep before the kids woke them at five-thirty A.M.

He groaned, and drove on.

Cathy Angel bit lightly into her lower lip. She'd seen Don's expression as he had moved on into the traffic, and it hadn't been encouraging. She'd pushed it, she decided. He didn't look good at all. In fact, he'd looked like Donald Duck as Mr. Scrooge in a Disney variation of the Dickens classic. Poor Don! He'd been working too hard lately. And she supposed she was making things pretty darn hard on him now. He always had a few different ideas about how a relatively young and childless couple should be spending the holidays.

And he always gave in to her.

Maybe not after this year. Not after the way he had looked at her.

Still, she had gotten everything she wanted. Christmas was the most special time of the year. Churches were so beautiful with their Nativity scenes, and the Christmas carols made her feel warm. Christmas Day . . . waking up to the children's excitement, sipping hot cocoa while the little urchins were allowed to open a few gifts before church. Neighbors greeting neighbors. For once in this hectic world, people stopping to talk to one another, to say "Happy Holidays."

Don would be happy, too, she assured herself. Once they reached her folks' home in Connecticut, he'd relax. He'd forget the pressures of work. He liked to pretend that he couldn't take too much of the kids, but he laughed as hard as she did over their antics and spoiled her nieces and nephews every bit as much as she did. He pretended he didn't enjoy the kids, but she knew no matter what he said, that was because it seemed she couldn't have children. They'd tried some of the high-tech fertility techniques, so far with with no luck. He'd flat-out refused to have anything to do with having a child with a surrogate mother. Though they'd been willing to try adoption, they'd tried all legal and legitimate channels, and they'd been assured that adopting an infant—even a young child—might take years.

Cathy would happily adopt an older child—any child, but she hadn't quite gotten Don to that point. Yet.

She smiled suddenly, even knowing what his mood was going to be. It might take a little time, but she'd get him around to her way of thinking. Eventually.

She didn't want him to have to go through any more traffic snarls so she hurried along Fifth Avenue carefully. She saw a Santa waving his bell over his donation pot, and though she'd already given to several that day, she dropped in a few dollars for this Santa—she thought they might have Santa-donation contests or the like and wanted to give all the Santas she passed an even chance. Just ahead, Don had managed to pulled the car over. Taxis and cars were honking as if they had lives and wills and voices of their own. She ran, determined she wasn't going to cause him any more problems. Poor

Don! He looked like such a thundercloud, and on Christmas Eve.

He opened the door as she neared the car. The ground was slick with rain over snow that the subway system exhaust hadn't quite managed to melt. Cathy slid the remaining few feet to the car, caught herself at the door, and threw her packages into the back seat. She dived into the front seat, ready to give Don a quick kiss on the cheek.

He turned his head toward the traffic, swearing as a taxi sped by. She arched a brow and decided against the kiss. "We should already be there by now," he said, "instead of fighting our way through this zoo. Look up there—the idiot must think he's a kamikaze pilot."

"I'm sorry. But really, tomorrow morning, being a little late tonight will be well worth it."

"A little late?" he inquired.

"I'm still glad we decided to work this morning. I finished the sketches for the Herrington house, and Herrington himself happened to walk in because he wanted to bring the studio employees chocolates for Christmas. He was absolutely thrilled with my designs for his Westchester house, and Frederick was so thrilled that he's given me a bonus two weeks off this year. I'll have five weeks vacation time. Isn't that wonderful?"

"Absolutely. I just may be off all year."

"What?" Cathy gasped. Startled, she stared at Don. He kept his eyes upon the road. He looked haggard, she realized unhappily. He was such a handsome man.

She'd always thought so. She'd seen him for the first time during her freshman year at Holy Cross. Wavy auburn hair, steady hazel eyes, one of those rugged, craggy profiles that made men look so sexy and appealing. She'd been halfway in love with him before she'd even met him. Their first date had been a football game. She'd discovered they were almost complete opposites—she was art, he was business, she was outgoing, he was quiet. The strong, silent type, she had determined. She was cheerful, he was grave. It hadn't mattered, or perhaps it had. Maybe they had fulfilled each other right from the start, providing what was lacking in the other. He still tended to the serious side, all these years later, and he was quick to tell her that she was terminally cheerful.

None of that mattered. She loved him now more than ever. He'd stood by her through so many things. She knew he never quite realized how wonderful she thought he was for the way he had stood by her in their efforts to have children, how grateful she was for the uncomfortable tests and efforts he had been willing to make.

Now he was silent. And very grim.

"Don, they couldn't possibly have fired you!" she said.

He was silent—that craggy profile still turned toward the road. Then he sighed. "No. No one fired me."

"Then . . . ?"

He shrugged.

"It just—sucks. This whole Christmas thing just sucks. The rest of the world is already off or in the middle of a party. I work my tail off—like I've been doing for weeks now—and the boss walks in and thinks energy makes me too young to be fit for an important job." He glanced at her at last. "They took the case from me, Cathy."

"Oh, Don!" she commiserated.

He turned off the Avenue, heading out for the freeway. Cathy noted that the traffic was getting not just heavier, but wilder. People trying to get around the escape-the-city crunch were just about driving along the sidewalk.

"We didn't have to go to work on Christmas Eve," he reminded her a bit bluntly.

"No. I'm sorry."

"We could have been in Aruba."

She lifted a hand in the air. "But Christmas is—"

"Snow and ice on the roads. Maniacs who would happily shoot you to get you out of their way."

"Mistletoe and holly, hot chocolate, sweet little squeals of delight when kids open a special package, dollars in little black kettles that just may make life sweeter for some unfortunate soul—"

"Who could get his butt up and work for a living, probably," Don interrupted.

"Don!"

He sighed, staring at the road ahead of them again.

"Cathy, I—"

"What?"

He shook his head. "Cathy—it's just wrong, what you do."

"I don't know what you're talking about."

"It's wrong, it's crazy, it's self-destructive. You go nuts over other people's kids at Christmas. When someone is pregnant, you buy her gifts and maternity clothes. As soon as a baby is born, you're there to gush over it. You're just hurting yourself." He stopped for a second, then finished, "You just hurt us both, this time, buying more silly gifts to stick under a Christmas tree for kids that aren't even our own."

She stared at his profile, stunned, hurt. Then she realized that he was the one hurting. Hurting for her as much as he claimed that she had just hurt them both.

"I'm okay, Don. Maybe I will never have a child, maybe we'll never even be able to adopt one. But I'm not hurting myself; I take pleasure in a friend having a baby—"

"It has to make you suffer!" he exploded.

She shook her head. "Of course, I wish it were me. But a baby is just precious, whether it's mine or not. A child is just precious. Oh, Don, I am really sorry, and you do have a right to choose how to spend Christmas, too. If you really want to go to an island next year and sit in the sun, we can do that. But I love to spend Christmas with my nieces and nephews. It doesn't hurt me. I'm okay, honest. And if—"

"What?" He shot a glance toward her.

"If those jerks don't appreciate you enough, you should just up and quit."

She saw his lips twitch. He started to smile.

"Cathy, I can't just up and quit. We bought a very expensive co-op apartment—"

"I have a good job."

"Yes, and you're an up-and-coming designer. You're going to have to make choices—you can't work knowing everytime you buck the system you're risking the roof over our heads and really succeed."

"Don, you'll get another job, you're a brilliant young attorney." She shrugged and grinned. "They can't hide your light under a bushel forever! Quit. Go somewhere else. I can cover us while you do it."

He stared at her hard. "Then what? What if a miracle occurred and we were able to conceive a baby? Or the perfect infant dropped out of the heavens? You wouldn't be able to stay home with our child, which is what you've always wanted."

She looked ahead. "You don't believe in miracles."

He lifted his hands from the steering wheel in aggravation. "No, I don't. Something is wrong with us and we can't—"

"Something is wrong with me," she corrected softly.

"Something is wrong with us," he insisted, "and we can't have children. That won't change. Do you think itsy-bitsy Christmas elves will pop down on you like snowflakes and permeate your skin to repair whatever isn't quite right in your reproductive tract?"

"Don!"

He exhaled, thinking what an ass he was. He shook his head. "I'm sorry, I'm just in a hell of a mood. I worked my butt off and all I got was a good kick in it! We're good people, with good jobs, and what happens? We can't do what the majority of murderers, rapists, and thieves can do easily—reproduce! Life sucks, and Christmas sucks big time."

"Don, Don, it doesn't!" Cathy said, twisting in her seat. "Dear God! Think of all we have that others don't! Think . . ."

He could hear Cathy talking, but not what she was saying. They'd cleared the city; they were approaching railroad tracks. He could hear the *ding-ding-ding* warning that a train was coming. He could hear the sound the train made, the great wheels turning, a sound every child knew.

The striped gate that closed to block the road when a train was coming had gone crazy, rising, falling, rising, falling.

The train was whistling.

And the sound . . . There was something wrong with the sound the train's wheels were making.

The cars were derailing, he thought.

He glanced in his rear-view mirror. Above the *ding-ding-ding* of the warning signal and the shrill whistling of the train, he could hear a mallardlike honking sound. Louder and louder. Lights, coming from the high beams of a mammoth truck, were shooting blindingly into his rear-view mirror.

Ding-ding-ding-ding—

Honk! Honk!

"Jesus!" he shouted suddenly.

The train was coming. And the driver honking behind him wasn't trying to be Christmas-obnoxious—*he had lost his brakes*. Within split seconds, the truck was going to send him flying into the train, then come crashing into it behind him. He couldn't yell, Cathy, duck! He couldn't calmly ask, Cath—you got your seatbelt on? He couldn't dart to his left because he was hemmed in. He couldn't slide to his right because of the snow plow sitting idle.

Whether they ducked, braced, or laced themselves in with a dozen seatbelts . . .

It wasn't going to matter.

He looked at her. His knowledge of what was about to happen was in his eyes.

Seconds. Split seconds. He'd heard a drowning man saw his life flash before his eyes as he went down. He didn't see the life he'd lived. He saw the little things he would miss. That rare robin's egg blue sky over the high-rises of Manhattan. His mother's corned beef, the rich, deep, aroma of his father's pipe tobacco. The sight and scent of fall in Central Park.

Cathy.

Cathy.

Cathy . . .

A little late to realize what an ass he'd been. Seconds were gone. Milliseconds . . .

"Oh-God-Cathy-I'm-so-sorry-I-love-you—I-love-you-so-much!" he cried.

Her eyes widened. She stared at him. She'd heard the train, but not the very different sound of it. She'd heard the truck horn, but she hadn't realized.

Dark blue eyes stared at him. Angel eyes, he had always thought. And "Angel" eyes, he had told her, after they had married. So huge now, so beautiful, so puzzled and concerned.

"Don, I love you, too," she began in confusion.

Then the truck hit.

The train let out a final ear-piercing whistle—then twisted from its tracks.

Trains, cars and people plummeted through the night.

For a second, there was silence.

All that could be heard were the strains of "Silent Night, Holy Night," coming from a car radio.

A light dusting of snow suddenly started to fall.

And then the screams began.

CHAPTER 1

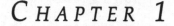

"Silent night, holy night . . ."

Dimly, dimly, he could hear the music. It came louder now, yet the music, the song was still so soft.

"All is calm . . .

"All is bright . . ."

No, nothing was calm. It was the night from hell. There was cacophony. So many screams, cries, groans . . .

"Cathy, Cathy!"

The impact was over. No more movement. Fire! He inhaled, smelled no gas. He couldn't see! he realized. He blinked. Something was in his eyes. Blood. Oh, God, he blinked again. Almost cleared his vision. Don went to unhook his seatbelt, trying to realize how he had become so cut up. No airbag in the old Beamer, he thought. He saw that the windshield had caved in.

His beige coat was drenched in something sticky and dark. Blood, he thought dizzily. More blood. Cathy. Oh, God, Cathy. He blinked again. Looked for her. Groped for her. Her head was bent forward. Glass fragments had rained over her hair. He reached for her, gently, thinking that he had to be careful, couldn't disturb her, the paramedics would be coming, police, doctors . . .

"The children, the children, all those babies!" someone was shrieking. There were screams again, cries, moans, broken sobbing. He couldn't think about those sounds. Cathy, Cathy, oh, God, Cathy . . .

And the cold . . . The cold was stealing over him even as he reached for her. He had to touch her. He didn't dare try to discover why he was drenched in blood. He touched her cheek, frantically crying her name.

"Cathy, please, oh, Lord, Cathy, please, don't, don't die, please . . ."

She stirred, slightly. Lifted her head.

Opened her eyes.

Angel eyes. Oh, Cathy. Oh, God, take me. Let her live—she has so much life, so much to give to everyone . . .

"Don," she said, barely mouthing his name. She smiled, but there was something in that smile. It was weak, wry.

And he knew.

God wasn't listening. There were no miracles.

She was dying.

And she knew that she was dying.

And being Cathy, she was grateful anyway. Grateful to see his face again, reach out and touch him once more.

"Don . . ."

There was so much darkness around them. The wreck had knocked out street lights. Headlights flared and died, blazed eerie patterns of illumination over the tragic accident. He saw her face; it disappeared. Saw it, lost it. Those eyes. Angel eyes.

"Cathy!" he found her fingers. Curled his own around them. He leaned toward her. Her door, damaged in the crunch, fell open with a horrible rasping sound. Cathy slipped from the car.

"No!" he cried, fighting the waves of frigid cold that were sweeping over him, stealing both his strength and his will.

Waves of death.

Yes, death.

How strange that he should know it so clearly, and with such absolute certainty.

It didn't quite matter what had occurred. Just what injury it was that soaked his coat in blood.

Oh, God, this was it, this was how it happened. Death was cold, Death was ice. Killing first the extremities, then the limbs, then the heart, the mind . . .

The soul?

With every effort, he dragged himself from the driver's seat, to the passenger's seat. Out the door.

He fell on her. Damned himself even in death as he heard the painful expulsion of her breath.

"Cathy . . ." He could hardly make a sound anymore. Tears stung his eyes. "Cathy . . . are we dying? Cathy, oh, Cathy . . ."

She looked at him and nodded. Winced. Sound went on around them, so distant, part of a different world. He brought his fingers to her again. Ten bloody fingers entwined. Someone was sobbing near them. He was dimly aware of what he heard.

"The children, the children, someone help me, they're in this car. Oh, dear God, the blessed little orphans, help, help, someone help them . . ."

Something huge and black passed by them. He thought that Death had swooped down for them then, quickly and neatly. But the huge black thing came and went, leaving a flurry of snow to fall down upon them, as if they were done for already. Don blinked. Not death, but a nun. Running across the metal-and-flesh-strewn accident scene. Trailing blood herself, trying to get help.

Sirens, so many sirens suddenly. So close.

So distant.

He held her right fingers, those on her left hand trailed into his hair.

"I love you. So much. Those poor little ones in the train. Don, oh, God, I had you, I had everything. No regrets, Don."

"Not even children?" he whispered bitterly.

She smiled. "I had you. I had so much. I can almost
. . . die happy."

"Don't say it, don't say it, dammit. Cathy, you can't
die—you can't—and you can't be happy—"

"We're together, Don." She inhaled. Her chest rattled
terribly. There was blood in her lungs, he thought. A
clinical realization. At such a time.

"Dying together," he told her. He wanted to sob, to
rail, to curse loudly and furiously.

Demand a miracle.

He hadn't the strength.

Nor the belief.

Cathy was talking. He wanted so badly to hold on to
her. He didn't even seem to be able to do that.

"But life was good. Listen to me, *I had you.*"

"You had an ass. I had you. Everything. Oh, God,
Cathy, help is coming, listen to me, sweetheart, you
have to hang on, you can make it."

"Cold, Don. So cold. Hold me."

He wanted to hold her. The cold had seized him. His
limbs. His torso. His heart, he was certain. He could
suddenly hear it beating. One thump. A very long time.
Another thump. Each beat coming more and more
slowly. Soon the pulse would stop completely.

"Touch me!" she whispered.

He couldn't feel her heart at all.

"Touch me!" she pleaded again. "Don, I can't! I can't!
I'm too cold to reach you. Please, touch me, reach me, let
me feel you one last time . . ."

He tried. Tried again. Dragged himself up.
He pressed his lips to hers.
And died.

Or thought he died. It was the weirdest damned night. He touched her, kissed her. The cold overwhelmed him, sweeping throughout the whole of him. But now . . .

Apparently, he hadn't been hurt that badly at all. He had been hallucinating.

He had his hands on a heavy luggage bin and was shoving it aside. There had been a railroad conductor beneath it, pinned there. The man was unconscious, but breathing evenly. He might have a broken leg, Don mused, looking at the position of the fellow's limb, but it looked like he had a good chance.

"Don, come here!"

He looked up. Cathy was standing at the cock-eyed entryway to one of the train cars that had gone askew. He hurried toward her. He looked down as he leaped over the wreckage and realized vaguely that the blood was gone from his trenchcoat. He didn't seem able to dwell on that for the moment; Cathy was calling him.

"Careful. Careful. There are a bunch of little ones trapped inside here, Don. Can you see?"

The train's lights had gone out. Only here and there were flashes blinking illumination. Don could still see that this railcar was the one loaded with children. The orphans. They had apparently come from a Brooklyn facility called St. Mary's: the name was stamped upon most of the clean, though shabby and worn, baggage the munchkins had carried; some had suitcases, some backpacks. The bags seemed to have come in a multitude of sizes, perhaps six or seven in all.

"Cathy, maybe we shouldn't touch them. Listen to the sirens. People who know what they're doing are coming now. We could hurt them—"

"Don, smell," she told him.

Hmmm. He didn't seem to be able to do that. But he thought he saw some smoke billowing in from the rear of the car.

"All right, let's get them out," he said to her. "There, I'll pull up that broken seat, you grab the youngster."

He heaved against a seat that had been twisted severely in the violence of the wreck. It appeared to have been bent as easily as a coat hanger. He pressed, strained. It wasn't going to move.

Then, to his astonishment, he lifted it with no effort whatsoever. Cathy reached down for the child trapped beneath it. A boy of perhaps ten. Not a skinny little tyke, either, Don thought. The orphans at St. Mary's were not eating so badly. Except, of course, he reminded himself, boys didn't necessarily gain a little weight from too much nutritious food.

"He must be heavy, Cath," he warned.

"Not at all," she told him. "Grab that sweet little toddler there. Two more trips and we'll have them all."

There were six of them, all boys, if Don could guess

correctly, between the ages of three and ten. They were smudged and dirty. Only three of them had stirred, groaned, or moved. He knew one had a broken wrist; another, well, he wasn't sure if the boy, a handsome, lanky, blond-haired lad of about nine, would make it. Yet he suddenly stopped thinking about the boy because he could see his own Beamer, the broken headlights of it jammed against the derailed car of the train.

There were mounds in the new-fallen snow beside it. Snow-covered mounds, with more snow falling upon them. In fact, as the sirens screamed in the night and rescue workers began to come running across the darkness, their flashlight beams wavering over the terrain, Don realized with a sinking sensation just what he was seeing becoming buried in the snow.

Himself.

And Cathy.

She was just in the act of laying down one of the children, the littlest one, a round-faced cherub of about three.

"Cathy."

"Isn't this little guy adorable, Don? He's breathing evenly, too, I'm certain of it. Wave to those ambulance attendants there, they can't possibly see the children, and I'm afraid the kids will freeze to death before they get help. I wish I knew more about medicine—"

"Cathy—"

"Hello, over here! Hey, someone come help!" Cathy called. "Are those fellows deaf?" she demanded.

"Cathy, look!"

"Yes, yes, I know—it's snowing. Those poor people. Do you think that they're de—"

"Cathy, I think they're us!" Don exploded.

"What?"

"I've got to see!"

He went running, tripping, scrambling over wreckage, baggage—even the nun, fallen from a sprained ankle.

Cathy came quickly after him. Until she reached the nun.

"Sister, can I help you?" she asked solicitously.

The nun sobbed quietly, trying to struggle to her feet. Cathy pulled her up. The sister screamed, unable, it seemed, to realize how she was being helped. She hopped about in the snow, looking around her, in front of her, behind.

She seemed to stare straight at Cathy, without seeing her.

She looked heavenward.

Then passed out cold.

"How strange!" Cathy said, just barely catching the nun and easing her back down. "We need help here so badly! This poor lady will freeze if—"

"She's a nun, God's going to help her first!" Don snapped. "Leave her for now, please, Cathy. Just get over here!"

She stared at the sister. "You'll be all right, help is coming, real help is coming!" she promised, then went running after Don. She moved so quickly that she slammed into his back when he tensed and stiffened.

"Get around here!" he said, pulling her forward.

"Easy!" she protested.

"Look!" he commanded.

"Where?" she asked.

"Down."

"Down . . . where?"

"There. In the damned snow!"

"Oh, God!" she gasped, seeing the bodies. "Those poor people. They're so hurt!"

"They're so dead!"

"Oh, dear, Don, you're right—"

"Cathy, aren't you listening? *They are us! You and me. Us, Cathy!*"

"They can't be."

"Look at them! They are!"

They stared at the ground together.

At the couple there.

He had fallen to her side. Their heads were together, his reddish hair and her ebony waves plastered in the whiteness of the snow. Their blood-stained fingers were laced together. They were as close as could be.

In death.

"It . . . it really is us!" Cathy breathed. "It can't be."

"It is."

"But it—it can't be. We're here."

"We're there, too."

"But . . ."

"Oh, God!" Don groaned.

"What's the matter with you! Don't you say that!" Cathy gasped.

"What, what? What did I say?"

"God. Just don't, er, speak his name like that. Not under the circumstances . . . don't you think?"

He stared back at her. Into her wide blue eyes.

"Under the circumstances?" he blazed back. He stared up, heavenward.

Bitter.

He stared back at his wife.

"Who the hell do you think put us into these circumstances."

"Don, dammit, don't say hell!"

"Hell, Cathy, then cut the dammit!" he exclaimed.

"Oh, my God" she protested, "you've done it now."

"I've done it! Done what?"

Then he realized. Something was happening again.

The accident scene was receding from around them. And they seemed to be rising. But they couldn't be. Because the white was becoming so dense. They were . . . in snow. That was it. The snow was getting harder. Falling with incredible speed. Blanketing all around them.

No, he realized.

Not snow.

Mist encircled them. Spinning, swirling, thickening.

They were rising.

Rising within it.

Into the clouds.

CHAPTER 2

"We're dead. We must be going to . . . heaven?" Cathy said, a tinge of hope in her voice.

"We can't be."

"Don, we saw our bodies. We are dead. We just need to understand what's happening now. I was always so afraid to die. I mean, I believed in God, in an afterlife, but I—I was always afraid, I didn't want to go alone. You know how I hate going places alone."

"You're not alone. I'm with you."

"Are you afraid?"

"Yes."

"Think we may be going to heaven?"

"I hope. Surely, we can't be going to . . . hell?" Don murmured. "I wasn't great, but I wasn't that bad."

"Do you think all our sins play out before us now like a motion picture?"

"I hope not."

"I think hell is down. And very hot," Cathy assured him. "You're not hot, are you?"

"No, no, but in all honesty, I wasn't that bad, but I'm not so sure I deserve heaven. Maybe I'm just rising by hanging on to your shirttails."

Cathy smiled. Her fingers curled around his. "What makes you think I was that good? But we're together, right?"

He nodded. "Maybe we'll just float for eternity," he said worriedly.

"I don't think so," Cathy said.

Because they had reached some kind of a strange landing.

It was worse than the Christmas Eve rush on Fifth Avenue.

The flooring was nothing but mist; none of the hundreds of . . .*creatures?* . . . rushing about on it seemed to notice, or to have any doubt of the solidity of what lay under their feet. And wings.

They looked like people. Maybe they were people. Except for the ones with wings.

"Wings mean angels, right?" Don whispered to Cathy.

"I think."

"Or birds," Don said.

Cathy elbowed him. "I think it's time to be very careful about what we say." Her fingers still laced with his, she looked around, turning them both in a full circle.

The cloud-landing seemed to stretch on forever in all

directions. There were corridors within it, all formed
from the same misty white stuff, and thousands of people—or angels or, as Don was thinking of them, *humanoid*-type creatures—were hurrying about. They all
seemed to be moving with purpose. Their appearances
varied greatly; many were dressed like Cathy and Don,
in winter coats and boots. Others' outfits made the gath-
ering look almost like a costume party. To Cathy's left
was a group in bikinis and cutoffs, to her right, a couple
in exquisite medieval dress, probably from around the
period of Henry II. There were people in caftans, evening gowns, tuxes, dungarees, flapper outfits from the
roaring twenties, T-shirts in tie-dye colors advertising
the Grateful Dead, anything, anything at all that might
be imagined. Those wearing the varied costumes
walked about with lists; they walked with purpose, they
stopped by the desks, they moved onward. They all
seemed incredibly busy.

I will wake up, Don told himself.

He stared toward a group of young men and women
who began to change position. They were rising on a
cloud-elevator, so it seemed, heading upward toward a
small mountain or hill in the midst of the mist. The
shape was rather rugged and craggy, as the face of a cliff
might have been on earth, but there the resemblance
ended. Magnificent colors seemed to shoot down from a
dazzling light atop the cliff. Silver, gold, exquisite, vital
violet.

Next to the crest, slightly lower, was a group of hills,

ever so slightly mist-shrouded, yet beneath the silver-white mist, the colors were all in shades of green and brown. Cathy tugged upon Don's coat sleeve suddenly, pointing out a man in a brown caftan, carrying a staff. He was surrounded by animals—lambs and lions, birds, snakes, puppies, ponies, and so forth. A large giraffe walked past the man.

"St. Francis?" Cathy whispered.

"I don't know. I'm sleeping, surely. Dreaming," Don insisted.

"It's magnificent!" Cathy whispered. She kept her grip on his shoulder, turning them both in a circle again to keep looking around. And even as they looked around, they saw again the very busy place where they stood, the plain, the level. It was like a United Nations building on the eve of a world summit, like an airlines office on the busiest night of the year. People, creatures—angels?—appeared and disappeared into the mist once again, some rising, some lowering, all with purpose. In fact, most of the humanoid creatures seemed to be constantly coming and going.

All but the ones with wings.

The winged beings were no more uniform in appearance than those creatures of these clouds who didn't have wings. They wore all manner of dress, some the soft, flowing stuff of biblical-angel pictures, others much more businesslike apparel, and they seemed to be the ones giving out directions.

Don was still turning about with Cathy, gaping, when he felt the tap on his shoulder.

They spun about together. Faced one of the creatures with wings. He was very tall, a good six-foot-three, and was dressed in striking contemporary evening wear. He was incredibly good looking. His hair was a sandy color, wavy; his eyes were a dark, piercing brown. He might have been a Hollywood hearthrob—except that he was sporting large, white, really beautiful, feathery wings. Almost as long as his body, they seemed to be threaded through with silver.

"Cathy and Don?" the man said.

Don held Cathy's hand more tightly. "We're the Angels," he answered.

The man sniffed audibly. "We'll see about that."

"Angel is our last name," Cathy said.

"Here, you are Cathy and Don," the man stated. He stared at Don, his eyes narrowing assessingly. " 'Angel' is debatable as of yet!"

"Oh, is that so? Just who the hell are you?" Don demanded.

"Shhh!" Cathy whispered to him.

The winged thing looked at her. "My name is Gabriel. And you," he said, addressing Don, "may very soon be known as nothing more than mud. Remember, sir, the laws of gravity. It's far easier to drop than it is to rise."

"Now, wait a minute—" Don began.

Cathy tugged at his hand.

"Mr. Gabriel—"

"Not 'mister,' just Gabriel."

Cathy glanced at Don. Gabriel? *The* angel Gabriel? Her look warned him that he had better start being very careful, right now.

"Gabriel," she said, addressing the winged heartthrob, "we're really very confused. We're . . . umm . . . dead, right?"

"Dead as door nails!" Gabriel assured her cheerfully.

"Are we in heaven?" Cathy asked carefully.

Gabriel shook his head, his smile somewhat malicious as he stared at Don.

"But we're not in hell," Cathy said.

Gabriel downright smirked at Don. "Not yet," he said insinuatingly.

"Well, then . . ."

"This"—Gabriel made a grand sweep with his hand—"is something of a halfway stop."

"Purgatory?" Don asked.

"You betcha," Gabriel said.

Don looked at Cathy. "This can't be the angel Gabriel, Cathy. They didn't say 'you betcha' back in biblical times."

"I didn't have the Versace suit back then either," Gabriel said, straightening his sleeves. "Christmas present," he told Cathy with a smile.

"It's very nice," she assured him.

"Wait a minute!" Don snapped. "A materialistic angel?" He and Gabriel just weren't on the same wavelength.

"Sometimes, material goods are necessary for visits to a material world," Gabriel told him. "What can we do? Times change. Angels came to Abraham on foot, I have flown in a cloud of brilliant gold light for many important messages. This is the twentieth century. I may be taking a Harley or a Beamer somewhere next." He shrugged. "Maybe a nice white stretch limo. We can appear as light, as a whisper, as the guy next to you at a subway stop. We have been interpreted by different men of different cultures in many different ways. Seraphim and Cherubim have been mighty warriors, ready to fight the unworthy from the gates of hell; they have been beautiful, radiant silver-light creatures as delicate and elegant and gentle as one can imagine." He suddenly seemed to lose patience. "Enough of this! What do you want, a road map? You're dead." He leveled a finger at Don. "And I'm in charge of your case here."

"Our case?" Don said.

Gabriel groaned. "You are just here on her shirttails, bud. So pay attention and learn some manners."

"I have plenty of manners!"

"Don!" Cathy snapped. She tugged on his hand until her nails dug into his palm.

"Ouch!" he protested, wondering why, if he was dead, his hand could still hurt so badly. "I have to be dreaming. I absolutely have to be dreaming."

Gabriel shook his head. "Not to be trite, sir, but at this moment I am afraid I can well be your worst nightmare."

Don looked at Cathy. She hadn't been paying attention to Gabriel's snide words. She was spinning around once again, staring at the fantastic busyness of this place. A group of darling cherubs flew past them, chattering in melodic voices. A very long, incredibly graceful angel, in biblical dress, flew by thirty feet from them, to come down in the midst of the bathing-suit and cutoff wearers.

"Now there's an angel," Don murmured to Cathy.

"Rafael," Gabriel said.

"Properly dressed," Don commented.

"And so magnificent!" Cathy murmmured. "There's so much, of course, that we've read, so much from the Bible, so much from fiction. So many stories from the Old and New Testaments, and so many writers adding on to them! Milton! In *Paradise Lost!*" she said. "He wrote about Satan, before his fall from heaven, loving a seductress named Sin, and from their union, they created Death."

"Milton, a man of incredible talent!" Gabriel said. "A remarkable man with words." He smiled at her. "But Death is not evil," he said gently. "Death comes to every man, woman, and child . . . and—"

Something suddenly brayed behind him, then knocked him forward. He turned impatiently to see a small, lost donkey. "Someone bring this creature to Francis, will you please!" Gabriel demanded.

A pair of little cherubs, naked and plump, suddenly

swirled down with incredible speed, plucking up the little donkey.

"I just hate it when the animals get lost!" Gabriel exclaimed. "Where was I?" he asked Cathy.

"We were on Death."

Don stared at them both. It might have been a singles' scene. The two of them chatting over cocktails.

"Death is part of life," he said simply. "Life is to be lived to the fullest, until it is taken away, as it must be from all men and women—and animals!—on earth. Satan, however, did have a tremendous fall from heaven I'm afraid. He was quite extraordinary, you know. But too proud." He stared directly at Don.

"I'm not proud—I'm in the middle of a nightmare," Don insisted.

"He's in denial," Gabriel told Cathy.

"Now I'm going to be psychoanalyzed?" Don demanded. "Do you have a supervisor?"

Gabriel crossed his arms over his chest, smiling grimly at Don. "There's only a 'One-In-Three' step higher than me, sir. And I think you'd best take a little time before pushing for an appointment that high."

"But—"

"Satan," Gabriel said rather swiftly, "was a favored creation of God, beautiful in many ways, but too proud to acknowledge God's love for his newer creation— man. And Satan fell, amidst revolt among the heavens, but in many writings you will find that the description of hell is the absence of God's love. The absence of love itself is enough to create hell. Don't you agree, sir?''

Another warning, Don thought. He had just a slim chance to stay with Cathy.

"Don!" Cathy whispered, begging him to keep silent. She was awed by everything around her, fascinated, happy, enjoying herself.

Enjoying old Gabriel.

"Cathy," Don murmured, hurt.

"We have to listen and find out what is happening," she said quietly to him.

"It's already happened," Don said dully. "We're dead."

"And together!" Cathy whispered poignantly.

"This is all just the beginning for you," Gabriel said. "And I am here to help you."

"Really?" Don inquired.

"Some do need help more than others."

Don started to speak. Cathy stamped on his foot. Then Don smiled politely and rephrased his words.

"So, then, just what *is* happening?" he asked.

Gabriel drew a feathered pen and pad from his coat pocket. "Your wife, sir, has led an exemplary life."

"Well I wasn't exactly Jack the Ripper," Don protested.

"Poor Jack!" Gabriel said, tsking as he referred to the list again. He stared up at Don. "Demented, ill!"

"Poor victims," Don muttered.

Cathy gasped. "Jack the Ripper! Oh, my God! Don,

we get to know things now! Gabriel, who was Jack the Ripper? I've always been dying to know. Montague Druitt, not the Prince, surely! Think of all the questions we can have answered now! Did creatures from another solar system come to ancient Egypt? Oh! Was there a conspiracy against President Kennedy, or did Oswald act alone? Jackie! How is she? She was such a lovely woman, I do hope—"

She broke off. Both Don and Gabriel were staring at her. Don cleared his throat, glad for once that he wasn't the one with the angel glaring at him.

"There isn't time for prying into the secrets of the world right now, Cathy," Gabriel informed her. "And you, Don!"

Apparently, there wasn't any way for him to be off the hook very long.

"Pay attention now, sir. If you're a very rich man and you give a large sum to a charity, it's good. If you're a poor man and you give what you can to a charity, it's much better. The rich man can afford it, the poor man cannot. Are you following?"

" 'The meek shall inherit'?" Don queried.

"Something like that. Cathy has never questioned Divine decisions. She, sir, has never lost faith."

Don looked down at Cathy. "I don't need an angel to tell me that my wife is wonderful," he said.

"Don, that was lovely. Thank you," Cathy said. "It was very sweet."

"And wise, at the moment," Gabriel said dryly.

"Hey!" Don protested.

"He always made me very happy, and stuck with me no matter what," Cathy said in Don's defense. About time, Don decided. She still smiled a little too easily at Gabriel.

"You're going to get a chance to be angels," Gabriel said.

"We are the Angels," Don told him.

"*Real* angels," Gabriel said without humor. "Perhaps you'd better come with me now, to my office. There's a lot you have to understand."

Don stared at Cathy, shaking his head. "The angel Gabriel has an office?"

Gabriel shrugged. "Fax machine, E-mail, you name it. I don't think you begin to understand the importance of my taking your case personally."

"We're very grateful," Cathy said.

"Ummm," Gabriel said dryly, his dark gaze on Don once again.

"All right, why is it so important?" Don asked.

Gabriel sighed, shaking his head impatiently. "Angels are messengers, of course, sir, but I am *the* messenger angel," he explained. "Don't you know any of the scriptures, Don?"

"Well, of course, I do—"

"I am the main messenger angel, the messenger of Christmas; and angels under my supervision are perhaps the most important angels. I brought the message of the greatest gift to the world; now Christmas angels bring the gifts of miracles to those who can believe. As your wife believes, Mr. Don Angel. Being a Christmas angel is an incredible honor, an honor which I am not at all personally sure you deserve. There are basically nine angelic orders, sir, surrounding Divinity—Seraphim, Cherubim, and Thrones topping the order; Dominations, Virtues, and Powers following upon the middle tier; then the Principalities, Archangels, and Angels. You are striving to reach the last rung of the tier, sir, yet there to be among the most important, designated Christmas angels, for it is the time of the year when God's Greatest Gift was given. Now come along. Follow me."

Gabriel turned. Cathy tugged at Don's hand again. He looked down into his wife's pleading blue eyes. "You've just got to be nicer to him."

"I'm being nice! He's the rude one."

"Don, he's also Gabriel."

"Right. I had a miserable day at the office, then a deadly accident kills me. Next, I get an angel with attitude to tell me what to do."

"Don, please, we're together!" Cathy reminded him.

He sighed. "Fine. I can be nice. I'm dreaming anyway. I know it. I have to be dreaming."

"What if you're not?"

"I have to be, I have to—"

"You have to be nice!" Cathy insisted.

"Right! I have to be nice. I have read the scriptures, you know. Well, some of them," Don admitted. "You can't just trust an angel blindly."

"You can't trust an angel?" she said doubtfully.

He straightened uncomfortably. "I remember something about a race of angels—giant, striking angels coming down and seducing the daughters of man."

"That was at the beginning of time, and they were supposed to be a tenth order of angels or the like."

"He is very good-looking."

"Why . . . you're jealous?"

"The thought of eternity with him around is just a bit unnerving."

"You have to take a good look at what I've seen so far!" she said, lowering her voice. "We're in a good place right now. Can you imagine if . . ."

Gabriel turned back to them. "Are you coming? Remember, the cloud you came in on can drop you down in a cloud of precipitation at any time."

"What does he mean by that?" Don whispered to Cathy.

"I don't know. I don't want to find out," she said. "Come on, let's follow him."

They hurried along the corridors. As they passed by a line of what must also have been "newly dead," Don felt a little shudder rip through him, along with gratitude that he and Cathy had been able to manage on their own after the accident. This lineup had not done so well. They were waiting below a sign that read REPAIR in large block letters. One poor fellow carried his head in his hands. Didn't seem to bother him, though. He was talking animatedly to the woman at his side who seemed to need her leg adjusted. Don didn't mean to stop and stare; he just did. The fellow with his head in his hands was gesticulating as he talked. Strangest damned thing Don had ever seen.

"Quit the gaping. Hurry along, now, I'm an extremely busy angel, and it is Christmas Eve on earth, you know," Gabriel said.

"Sorry, old chap," Don said. "You're really busy tonight, too, huh? And I thought you were called in on only the really big things."

Cathy jabbed him.

Gabriel stared at him. He smiled pleasantly. "No, Sometimes I get the riffraff as well. Now, are you coming with us?"

"Don—" Cathy began.

"I'm right with you," her husband said, his smile every bit as pleasant as Gabriel's.

Cathy and Don followed along. They were led through a snow white doorway into an office containing a very handsome antique desk topped with the latest in executive equipment. Gabriel gestured toward the two leather-bound chairs before the desk, seating himself in the swivel chair behind it. Cathy and Don sat. Gabriel folded his hands before him on the desk.

"Are you quite ready?" he asked.

Cathy nodded. Don folded his own hands before him. "I'm all ears," he said.

"That can be arranged," Gabriel warned.

Don smiled, grating his teeth. "I'm listening," he said.

And Gabriel began to talk.

CHAPTER 3

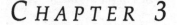

"Now that we're out of the Christmas mayhem around us, I'll try to be succinct and to the point. Wings must be earned. Again I tell you, there is no greater honor than being selected to be a Christmas angel, but no one—I repeat, no one—" Once again, he was staring at Don.

With that damned attitude again, Don was convinced.

"—becomes a Christmas angel without earning his or her wings. I may assume that my information is all correct, that you had a good marriage, that you do want to stay together throughout eternity?"

"Yes, definitely," Cathy said.

Gabriel arched a doubting brow to her.

"Now, dammit—" Don began.

"Don!" Cathy said firmly.

"I just don't know what the hell I ever did to offend this bas—"

"Don!"

He smiled around his clenched teeth once again, staring at Gabriel. "I wish very much to stay with Cathy throughout eternity. I am eager as all hel—"

"What he's trying to say is we're both very anxious to earn our wings," Cathy cut in quickly.

"Yes, that's it. Exactly," Don said.

"Listen to the rules," Gabriel said matter-of-factly. "Wings are earned through the completion of three Christmas miracles each. You have the power of suggestion, the power to move objects, the ability to appear and disappear at will. Do you understand?"

"Sounds like we're Christmas ghosts," Don said. "You know, 'Christmas past, Christmas future, Christmas present.' "

Gabriel offered him a very stern look.

Don tried very hard to return his stare without expression. No sense of humor here, that was certain.

"You haven't accepted the gravity of your own death, sir," Gabriel warned him.

"We're trying," Cathy said. "It was just so sudden. You know, one minute you're concerned with traffic and the day-to-day problems and then suddenly . . ." —she paused, looking at Don, smiling ruefully—"suddenly none of the little things matters at all. Not time, not traffic, not a dozen things that might have been important, irritating. Nothing on Earth matters."

Don's throat tightened. He wound his fingers more tightly around Cathy's. He looked at Gabriel. It had to be a dream, he kept telling himself. He'd been conked on the head damned hard. He was hallucinating.

He was dead! A damned dead man. Did dead men have hallucinations, or was this really death?

"Things still matter," he said. "People matter, Cathy matters—"

"Which is why you're being given a chance," Gabriel said, riffling through the papers on his desk. "Okay, were you paying attention? Three miracles each, three supernatural powers that will remain with you at all times—you can appear and disappear at will, you can move objects through simple mental effort, and you have the power of suggestion, do you understand?"

"Yes, I think so," Cathy said.

"I'm lost," Don admitted.

"You would be."

Don determined to ignore Gabriel. If this was purgatory, then Gabriel had a boss.

A Higher Power he had to answer to.

Don held his temper and asked evenly, "How do we know what miracles we're supposed to perform, and for whom?"

"It's all in your list," Gabriel said.

"Our list?"

"The one I'll be giving you soon."

"Of course."

"The miracles must all be accomplished by the stroke of midnight," Gabriel said.

"Six *miracles* between us by midnight?" Cathy said.

"Don't worry. You won't be expected to find the cure for a terminal disease or to bring peace to the world. But little miracles can be just as important as big ones," Gabriel assured her. "Remember, every single man, woman, and child out there is important in God's eyes."

"Well, yes, of course—" Cathy began.

"Little miracles," Gabriel said. He lifted his hands as if seeking a better explanation. "Christmas gifts." He leaned forward. "Making something work out for people who just keep trying and believing against all odds. That is a miracle, you see. When all facts and figures suggest that something just can't happen—but it does. When *faith* makes something happen. Do you understand? Well, if not, you'll learn as you go along. No one starts out perfectly."

"That's a relief," Don murmured.

"More rules," Gabriel said. "You can each call on me once. Just once. And only if absolutely necessary. I can't tell you how busy I am tonight. And I've a huge party tomorrow, you know."

"We go by our list," Cathy said. "We can each call on you once, we can appear and disappear, we have the power of suggestion and the power to move inanimate objects."

"Very good," Gabriel said.

"What happens if we don't succeed?" Don asked.

"Then you'll be judged."

"By . . . ?"

"Need you ask? May I simply suggest that you succeed?" Gabriel said, very politely.

"Is there anything else we should know?" Cathy asked.

To Don's surprise, Gabriel hesitated. "I'm afraid it's necessary that I warn you . . . especially you."

For once, Don noted, Gabriel was staring at Cathy. The warning was specifically for her.

"Warn us about what?" Don asked.

"Remember, nothing is perfect," Gabriel muttered. "You have a power . . . Well, you each have the power, once, just once, to give back life itself. But you mustn't do it."

"What?" Cathy gasped. "You mean, if someone is mortally injured—"

"If someone is stone-cold dead," Gabriel interrupted, "you have the power to give back life to that person."

"Do you mean we could even bring back to life someone who has been buried for years?"

"I certainly wouldn't. What a mess. Haven't you ever read 'The Monkey's Paw'?"

"But you just said—"

"Yes, I did. I said you have the power to bring life back. Once each. But you mustn't do so. If you do, you risk eternity."

"And damnation," Don said lightly. To his discomfort, Gabriel did not correct him. He was still staring at Cathy with stern concern.

"If you use that power, I can almost guarantee that you will not receive your wings. You will no longer be a candidate for eternity as a Christmas angel." He lowered his voice. "And again, no pun intended, God alone knows what will happen."

"I don't understand this," Don said. "If we're not to use the power—"

"Perhaps it has something to do with man's free will," Gabriel said. "I don't know everything," he added impatiently. "Just bear in mind that though you have the power, you have it once. Only once. And using the power can cost you absolutely everything you do have. Each other. Your future for all eternity. Now, have I explained it all to you clearly?"

"Clear as . . . mud," Don said lightly, and smiled to Gabriel.

Gabriel didn't crack a grin. He pressed a paper toward Don. "Sign on the dotted line."

"Sign on the dotted line?" Don demanded incredulously.

"Yes, sir, you heard me!"

"I have to be hallucinating!"

"Seconds are ticking away on Earth," Gabriel reminded him politely. "And you only have until midnight."

Being an attorney, Don immediately picked up the

paper to read it. It seemed to be an explanation of all that Gabriel had just told him.

A disclaimer?

Exactly. By signing, he and Cathy accepted all possible repercussions should they fail to follow the rules.

"You know, there is print on this contract so small an owl with a magnifying glass couldn't possibly read it."

"I hadn't noticed," Gabriel said.

"Don," Cathy murmured, "I don't think this is one of those occasions when we really have a lot of choice."

"May I have your—" Before Don could say the word *pen*, a handsome white feather quill floated before his hand. He plucked it from the air and signed his name on the paper.

Cathy took the paper and added her signature, beneath his.

Don felt as if they were buying a used car. He tried to tell himself again that he had to be hallucinating, dreaming, or the like.

But he'd seen himself—seen himself dead.

"Let me get this straight. If I find some poor kid about to drop dead from cancer on that list, I'm supposed to perform a miracle—but I can't give him life."

"On the contrary, you *can* give him life," Gabriel said.

"Well, hel—"

"Don," Cathy grated.

He inhaled. "Then I am confused."

"You *can* give him life. You've the power to do it. It's

simply that you must not do it. It may well be your own soul you lose in return."

"Then what good am I?" Don asked.

"Life—on Earth—only lasts so long for any man, woman, and child. It's a gift, like any other. And quite fleeting at the very best, against the spectrum of time. But there is a quality to every man's life. Life is a gift to be used to the fullest, no matter how the days are measured. Perhaps life itself is the greatest gift, but sometimes it takes a miracle to make people see that. You'll know more once you two get started. Ready?"

"Definitely. Christmas Eve is ticking away," Cathy said.

"But," Don began, "I still don't understand . . ."

"You may never understand," Gabriel said pointedly.

"Now, dammit, are we going to go through all this sh—"

"We are ready!" Cathy said, cutting him off.

He inhaled. Exhaled. Smiled at Gabriel. "Thanks. Thanks so much for the warm and friendly help. Glad to have you in my corner!"

Gabriel stood, staring down at the two of them. He offered Cathy his hand. She took it.

"Things will come to you. You'll see."

"I'm certain," she agreed.

"And remember, you can each call on me once. Only once, though, so make sure it's when you really need help."

"I understand," Cathy said.

Gabriel handed her a folded sheet of ivory paper and a very small book. "Your lists," he told her. "And a little manual in case you forget anything or have problems. Now, come along. I'll do my best to get you started off in the right direction."

Don stood quickly, pulling Cathy's chair back from the desk so that she could rise more easily. Since Gabriel was already starting out of the office, Don looked at Cathy and shrugged. She gave him a stern warning glance in return. "Yeah, yeah, yeah," he muttered. "It's a nightmare. I'm telling you; it has to be."

"If it were, wouldn't we have gone straight to hell?" Cathy asked.

"It's an imaginative nightmare," Don said.

"Yours or mine?"

"Mine."

"Why am I having it, too?"

"Because you're merely in the middle of my nightmare," Don explained, looking at her and not at where he was going. He crashed straight into Gabriel. The angel had stopped to wait for them.

"Will you get off my feet, please?" Gabriel demanded.

"Sorry," Don said stiffly.

"You two are dawdling away precious time," they were warned.

"No, no, we're on our way," Cathy said.

Gabriel took her elbow and led her to a small rise in

the cloud formation. Don came quickly around her other side and stood next to her.

He took her hand.

"Ready?" Gabriel asked.

Cathy nodded.

"You'll do fine," Gabriel assured her.

"Thanks," Cathy said.

"Just remember to do your best to keep that ass in line." Gabriel lifted a hand in farewell.

"Hey, now, wait a damned minute!" Don protested.

But Gabriel was already walking away, hurrying back along the corridor, having dismissed them completely. And their little patch of raised cloud was now moving at a swift pace downward.

"Don, you've really got to stop with the 'hells' and 'damns,'" Cathy warned nervously.

"*Ass!*" Don exclaimed incredulously, barely hearing her. He stared down at her. "Did you hear that? He just called me an ass! An angel can't say that, can he?"

Cathy quirked a brow at him, a half-smile playing upon her features. "I guess he can," she said. "He just did."

CHAPTER 4

Sharon O'Connor stared into her oven, at her rapidly crisping turkey.

She could feel her father standing not far behind her, in the kitchen doorway.

She closed her eyes tightly. Please God, she prayed in silence, please make Jimmy come home now. I know it would be a small miracle, but please let Jimmy come home, and let him come home sober.

"Thought you said Jimmy was coming home early for Christmas Eve dinner," her father said.

Sharon straightened, working a little pain out of her back as she did so. She turned the oven to off, deciding it was going to be a minor miracle if the bird was edible. She'd started turning the heat down on it bit by bit almost three hours ago when she'd first realized that Jimmy wasn't going to make it home around noon, when his office was supposedly closing for the day.

"He should be here soon, Dad. The traffic is so bad and all."

Her mother, Sharon realized, was standing beside her father. "Yeah," she heard her father mutter, "the traffic at Mulligan's strip joint and bar."

"Shh! She'll hear you," her mother said.

"She ought to hear somebody," her father muttered. He walked away, going back out to the parlor to talk to Timmy and Laura.

Sharon set her hand, fingers outstretched, over her expanding stomach. This one was another boy. Due on February fifteenth. That would make them a family of five. Just what they had planned. On paper, it was all perfect. They'd been married nearly ten years. They had an eight-year-old son, an adorable four-year-old daughter, and an infant boy on the way. They had their own house, a modest home, but a warm one not far from the Common, which they'd managed to keep no matter what Jimmy had lost through his gambling and drinking. They'd hung on to it because she'd worked hard making and selling custom clothing for infants, children, and women, and she'd kept their mortgage money separate from everything else.

It was so strange. Jimmy's drinking hadn't seemed so bad when they had first met. He'd been twenty-two, she'd been twenty, and a junior at Boston College. Jimmy had been a Harvard man. From the very beginning, she'd been crazy about him, and the more she had seen of him, the more deeply she had fallen in love with him. He was the most wonderful man she'd ever met. He planned to be an architect, he was brilliant, he was wild, and he was fun. He'd serenaded her dorm room one night, had presented her with a diamond engagement ring while kneeling in three feet of snow.

Jimmy O'Connor was from an affluent family who could trace their roots back to the sixteen-hundreds. They had produced doctors, lawyers, architects, writers, and PhDs by the score. At twenty-two, Jimmy had been gorgeous, with just a touch of red in his sandy hair, bright green eyes; tall, lean, with the quickest, sexiest damn smile in the world. He was popular, always surrounded by friends. And girls. That he had found Sharon attractive at all had amazed her—she was shy, quiet, almost reclusive, working class all the way. She'd made Boston College on a scholarship, and she'd known all her life that she'd have to keep up her grades to stay in school. Jimmy attracted a "play" crowd—adventurous, buxomy women. She was reserved and slim rather than curvaceous. When he'd asked her to marry him, she hadn't believed he could want her.

Their honeymoon had provided her with some of the most wonderful days a woman could imagine. Italy first, long nights drifting down the canals of Venice with a bottle of champagne towed behind the gondola. But then there had come the night when he'd gotten involved tasting wine with the owner of the small *pensione* where they had elected to stay.

He hadn't come back to their room until five in the

morning. She'd waited up. They'd argued. He'd told her that she had married him, not taken him prisoner. Naturally, she'd been hurt. She'd never wanted to make anyone a prisoner.

She hadn't realized she was becoming one herself.

There were still good times. Jimmy could be a wonderful father. That was one of the reasons she held on so tightly. But there were the bad times.

He'd been fired from his first job after they'd been married four years. The boss had claimed Jimmy was brilliant but unreliable. He showed up for work late. He disappeared too often at lunch.

Jimmy said the boss was a stuffed shirt, jealous of anyone who was capable of having a drink and a laugh.

He'd found a new job. A good job. And for a while, he'd been punctual and responsible. He'd been more shaken up than he cared to say by his firing.

That job had lasted three years.

Once again, he'd found employment. A Harvard degree could still talk, and the O'Connor name meant something in the Boston firms.

How long this job would last, Sharon didn't know. Her fingers shook as she placed them on the mound of her stomach. Her baby. Their baby. It was strange. She still loved Jimmy very much. The evenings he'd come home late, reeking like a brewery, he'd always tell her he knew when to stop. He'd been fired twice, but he was convinced that he didn't have an alcohol problem. A few times, when she'd known where to find him, he'd been in the midst of an admiring crowd—men and women. He didn't cheat on her, he assured her, and he couldn't help who hung around him, he had never hurt her, never taken a hand to her, though he had come close upon occasion. She tried to tell herself that if he'd ever hit her, she would have walked out.

But she didn't know that for certain.

"Mommy?"

She looked to the kitchen doorway. Laura stood there, a worn Teddy bear in her little fingers, her green eyes wide; Jimmy's eyes, very big.

A huge tear rolled from one of them. She inhaled on a ragged little sob.

"Grandpa said we should just go ahead and eat— Daddy might not be coming home. He will come home, right?"

Would he? Yes! He had promised! Did he forget his promises? Yes. Someone at the office had probably given him a drink. Someone single, unattached. Someone ready to drink and laugh through the evening, someone not burdened with children and a pregnant wife. Someone who was not a prisoner.

"Mommy? Will Daddy come home?"

"Silly thing! Of course, he will!" Sharon said. "Run on back into the parlor and keep grumpy old Gramps company, huh? Daddy will come home."

He had to. He had to . . .

She had to believe that.

Even if, at this point, she was reaching blindly for miracles.

Maggie St. Johns moved blindly along the street, trying to keep warm. She paused under a streetlamp, looking toward some of the fine homes on the street. Peering into the windows.

So many Christmas trees! So many children, so much laughter, so much light.

Once . . .

Once she'd been a child. Loved by two parents. So long ago. Her parents were gone now. No brothers, no sisters. She had cousins, surely, aunts and uncles. People who wanted to forget her, as the world had forgotten her.

Once . . .

Once she'd been beautiful.

She'd wanted to be a teacher. She could remember so very well. She had loved children. She'd been bright, cheerful, vivacious. Popular. Boys had loved her. The tall, handsome quarterback of the football team had been crazy about her. She'd married him right out of high school, forgetting about college and teaching because she was going to have a baby. She lost it. The tall, handsome quarterback became a crack-smoking lug. He beat her. She left him. She had so little talent and she was so young. She met a man, a rich man, and she fell in love, but he had a wife. The man convinced her to stay with him anyway, but he, too, became abusive, though he kept her because it was his right, he told her. And they fought. Then she was out on the streets.

Next, it was the customers who beat her. And as the years went by, only remnants remained of the beauty she had once had in such abundance. The customers who beat her forgot to pay her.

So she drifted.

And she dreamed . . .

And Christmas hurt, because she could still remember when she had been a beautiful child and the world had lain before her like an unopened present.

And someone had loved her.

She looked to the sky above her, smiled because she thought she saw a shooting star.

She didn't blame God for her present situation. She didn't blame anyone. She wondered if she could still dig her way out of her homeless and penniless situation. She touched her cheeks as she watched the star streak across the heavens, and she wondered if she could ever be beautiful again.

It didn't matter.

She looked back into a window in which a Christmas tree glimmered.

" 'Star light, star bright, first star I see tonight!' " she whispered, " 'I wish I may, I wish I might, have the wish I wish tonight.' "

She hesitated. "Merry Christmas, Lord!" she whispered. Then she smiled, and alone, in the shadows, she was beautiful once again. "Christmas . . . I just wish for the miracle of Christmas, Lord. With people. With lights, with laughter.''

Maggie started walking once again. It was too cold to stand still for long. She wondered if she could find a place to weather out the night.

Or if she would freeze to death by morning.

"Where are we?" Cathy asked. The mist that had encircled her was receding. She could hear cars, horns, a deluge of traffic. Lights streamed around them.

"In a pile of cold and snow," Don said, tromping on the ground to clear his shoes of some of the fine dusting of snow that had fallen.

Heavenly mist had become earthly snow.

"Boston!" Cathy said excitedly. "Look, there's the Common. I always loved this city. Little Italy, Quincy Market, the Aquarium—"

"Cathy, we're not on vacation," he reminded her softly.

"Right," she murmured dryly, "so don't you think we ought to enjoy any place when we get the chance?"

"You've got a point. You've also got the list."

"Ah!"

Cathy dug into her coat pocket, where she'd dropped the small book Gabriel had given her and the all-important ivory vellum list.

"Well?"

"We each have a miracle here, in Boston."

"Go on."

"You're to find a man named James Michael O'Connor."

"And?"

"And make him go home for Christmas Eve dinner."

"What's the catch?"

"He's in the middle of a crisis—a drinker in denial, with a worried wife, two children, and one on the way. Dislikes his in-laws because they see what's going on when his wife tries to cover for him. He loves his wife, but thinks no one understands him, believes he's a guy and just has to do guy things."

" 'A guy and he has to do guy things'?" Don repeated.

"Yes?"

"That's on the list?" Don said incredulously, arching a brow.

Cathy nodded.

"He's my miracle?" Don said.

"Right."

"And yours?"

"I need to find a homeless lady named Maggie St. Johns and find her a home for Christmas."

Don shook his head. "That's easy, compared to dealing with a drunkard."

"Oh, right! Get a family to open their door to a scruffy bag lady on Christmas Eve!"

"Gabriel likes you better."

Cathy started to speak, decided she couldn't argue that. Poor Don. His feelings were hurt.

Don threw up his hands. "This just can't be real."

"We're in Boston, right?"

"Yeah."

"We landed from a cloud, didn't we?"

He offered her a grimace. "I still say your miracle is easier than mine."

She smiled. "We're in this together, remember."

Don didn't smile in return. "Only if we can manage these miracles!" he reminded her.

She squeezed his fingers. "Piece of cake."

"Keg o' beer!" Don countered. "I think I found where we're supposed to start."

A neon sign, garishly strewn with Christmas lights, advertised MULLIGAN'S PUB & FINE DINING ESTABLISH-MENT.

"Think he's in there?"

"I imagine that's why we're on this corner."

"Shall we, then?"

Don hesitated. The place looked downright seedy. "I'm not at all sure I should take you in there."

"I always wanted to see the inside of a place like that."

"What?"

"I've only seen joints like that in movies!" she said with a laugh. "I'm curious. Oh, Don, what could possibly happen to me? I'm already dead!" she reminded him.

"Yes, but . . ."

"I'm not going to strip and dance on a table or anything."

"Promise?"

She elbowed him in the ribs. For a dead person, she had quite a punch.

"Let's get on with your miracle," she said firmly.

To Don's distress, Cathy headed quickly for the doorway. He followed her, wanting to make sure that she didn't enter the place alone.

He hated to admit it, but at one time, before he'd met Cathy, he had lived a slightly wild life.

He'd done a few of those "guy things" himself.

But he'd never been in a place like this one.

"Wait a minute," he told Cathy.

"Yeah."

"Maybe we should go in as invisible. Check that little book of yours and see how we do it."

Cathy pulled out the book; flipped through the pages.

"How do we do it?" he asked.

She shrugged. "Just *think* invisible."

"You're kidding me."

"I'm not."

With a groan and a shake of his head, he *thought* invisible. People seemed to be walking by, not noticing them. He could still see Cathy, but he hoped they were supposed to be able to see one another.

With a shrug, he opened the door for her, then decided they must be invisible, because a man came along behind them, shivering, and closed the door more tightly once they had entered the small and crowded foyer. Don took her hand and led her past a small reception stand. She collided with his back as he stood dead still, staring.

It was a medium-sized place. Really something like a local pub. Except for a long bar with three little curved areas that jutted out around the tables. Each one of the curves sported a pole, and each pole was decorated by a woman in various stages of undress—who danced to the beat of the music that pulsated through the room.

"Not bad looking—the dancers—for a sleazy place like this."

"You noticed?" Cathy said.

"It's a 'guy' thing," he told her. "There are some empty seats over there."

"Which guy do you think is O'Connor?" Cathy asked as they moved across the room.

The question was answered for them as a heavy-set man suddenly called out, "Jimmy! Jimmy O'Connor! Merry Christmas, my man. Buy the boy a drink, Mercy!" he told the waitress. He slapped his hand against the back of a man just around a bar curve from Cathy and Don.

Jimmy O'Connor.

He was wearing a nice suit—one Gabriel might well approve, Don thought—but it was a little crumpled. O'Connor had loosened his tie, and his hair, which he wore a little long, hung around his face now. He was a handsome man, quick to smile.

A young man, still.

But the first signs of dissipation were beginning to appear. His cheeks were just beginning to sag a bit, and his flesh was acquiring a ruddy tinge. He needed a shave. He smiled at the fat man buying him a drink.

"Thanks, Harry," O'Connor told the fat man.

"Whatcha doing out on Christmas Eve, a married fellow like you?" the fat man asked.

Jimmy shrugged. He lifted the shot glass of whiskey before him to salute the fat man, swallowed it down. "Just stopped by for a quick one. And to give Angela her Christmas tip."

Angela was a dancer. Very busty . . .

"Limber," Cathy commented to Don as Angela dipped the lower portion of her body toward Jimmy, who slipped a bill into the very thin strip of elastic still holding a feather in a strategic location.

Don lost what Jimmy was saying next because Cathy added, "She really is a very good dancer. I always wished I could do that."

"Dance with a pole?"

She smiled. "Dance . . . sexily like that. Don't you remember Jamie Lee Curtis in *True Lies*? She was spectacular. I didn't want to have to dance with a pole for a living or anything—I would just have liked to have been that sexy for you."

"You were sexy as sexy could be."

"Not that sexy."

"The sexiest."

"Really? You're not just saying that? I was your wife, you know," Cathy said skeptically.

"To me, you were the sexiest creature alive."

"We did have a good life, didn't we?" Cathy asked.

"We did." he said. *And I realized it far too late,* he thought, but he didn't say so out loud.

"He's heading for the john," Cathy said suddenly.

"Who?"

"Jimmy O'Connor! Your miracle boy."

"So what? You want me to follow him?"

"Of course. You have to keep an eye on him. Maybe you can help in there."

"Help him what? Pee?" Don demanded.

She shook her head. "Power of suggestion. Go play on his mind."

"Cathy—"

"Do you want me to go?" she demanded.

Don swore. Cathy kicked him. He stared at her, shaking his head. "I'm a dead man in a strip joint on Christmas Eve, and you want me to watch my language?"

"Just go!" she commanded.

CHAPTER 5

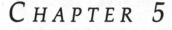

With Don gone, Cathy drummed her fingers on the table. Christmas Eve, she thought, was slipping away. She drew out their list again and read about her own first "Christmas Miracle." She needed to find a homeless woman named Maggie St. Johns.

Boston was a big city. And, unfortunately, there were far too many homeless people in it.

Lots of drunks, too, but they'd found Jimmy O'Connor easily enough. She drummed her fingers. She didn't dare call on Gabriel for her first miracle. She drew out the little instruction book and turned to page one and read, "Always look for the obvious. Always make good use of coincidence; remember that the right set of coincidences can be miracles all on their own."

Look to the obvious . . .

She glanced toward the men's room, then slipped from her bar stool and hurried toward the front door of the pub. She thought she bumped into a man, but he didn't notice; he walked right by. She bit into her lower lip, realizing that he had walked right through her.

She was dead. Really dead.

The thought made her want to cry; they'd had so much more left to do! It didn't matter, she realized. She had tonight. Tonight to make sure that she and Don could stay together throughout eternity. How strange! She'd been so lucky; she'd always loved her husband. Now, when he was groping a bit to deal with this, she loved him all the more. She'd always been a fighter, and now she was fighting for all eternity.

She stood outside in the dusting snow, looking both ways, up and down the street. The night was growing quiet, but she thought she saw movement way down the street. She stood very still, watching. Someone bundled up in a threadbare coat was tentatively checking out the garbage behind a donut shop. There seemed to be nothing there.

The badly dressed woman started walking again. Very quickly, Cathy thought, as she started across the street. A huge moving van came trundling along, and Cathy stepped back before she remembered that there wasn't much the truck could do to her anymore.

When she crossed over, the woman had nearly disappeared down the street. Cathy started to run after her.

Seconds later, she was amazed to discover how winded a fledgling angel could become. She gripped a streetlamp, inhaling, exhaling. She stared at the house in front of her and read the name on the very American red-white-and-blue eagle-shaped mailbox.

O'Connor.

Look to the obvious.

Far down the street, the woman who had poked through the donut-shop garbage had slowed down. She was looking at the bright Christmas lights attached to the handsome residences here by the Common. Looking into windows. At Christmas trees.

The power of suggestion was hers, Cathy had been told. She simply hadn't been informed how to use it.

She looked down the street, concentrating. *Come back, Maggie. Come back and see this house.*

She looked toward the dwelling. *Come out, Mrs. O'Connor. Come and look for your husband.*

It didn't seem to be working. Maggie was still moving away. The O'Connor's door remained closed.

Come look for your husband!

I don't have a husband. I left the abusive slug years and years ago!

Cathy muttered a swift curse, realizing as the thought-reply came flying back at her from Maggie that she'd been sending her power of suggestion in the wrong direction that time.

Try again. She was allowed a few screwups, really. She was new at this.

Maggie, come back this way. Come back, Maggie. Come and look into the warmth of this house . . .

To Cathy's surprise and relief, Maggie turned at last,

shaking her head in confusion as she looked back over the street she had just walked down.

Maggie began to walk toward the O'Connor house. Slowly at first. Then more quickly. She stopped at last beneath the streetlamp just to the side of the front of the O'Connor house.

What was he doing here on Christmas Eve? Jimmy wondered, stepping into the men's room of Mulligan's. Considering the place, the atmosphere and all, the facilities were fairly decent. There was a broad mirror over the three sinks, a line of three urinals, a row of three stalls. He walked straight for the urinals, his kidneys loaded. After absently unzipping his fly, and relieving himself, he closed his eyes, leaning against the wall. He should have had beer, not whiskey. He'd wound up with whiskey and beer chasers.

He should have gone home.

He didn't know why he hadn't. Except that he'd wanted a drink. And when he drank at home, even if it was Christmas, everyone stared at him. Like he was doing something wrong. Even Sharon didn't say a word. She just looked at him.

She never said a word. No matter what he did. When he'd gotten fired, she'd just spent more time in her sewing room. When he stayed out late, she just took the kids with her wherever she went. No matter when he came in, she had dinner ready if he was hungry. He wondered briefly if the way she so unquestioningly loved him was why he had decided to marry her. Or had he just proposed because she was different, a challenge. Sharon Challifour, so solemn, so studious! Seducing the girls who hung around him had been no challenge. Getting Sharon into bed had been a notch in the old belt.

Oh, sweet Jesus, he was thinking about his wife. His pregnant wife. Mother of two already. She'd been lucky to marry an O'Connor of Boston.

Lucky to marry him.

Hell, no! Poor damned Sharon—why the hell hadn't she left him yet?

Better still, just what the hell was he afraid of, huh? Getting old? Making real commitments? Facing the truth about himself?

You're not a great O'Connor of Boston, Jimmy. You're just a drunk. A drunk. If it weren't for your name and your family, and a wife who picks up your sodden carcass every time you go on a bender, you'd be on the streets, no better than the bums who huddle in the gutters . . .

Bull. He wasn't a drunk. That was what his hardworking, long-suffering in-laws wanted him to believe. He just wanted a good time now and then. Angela was a good time, this place was a good time. Just a drink, a few laughs, a little provocation . . .

He opened his eyes, amazed that, even with all the whiskey and the beer chasers, he could still be peeing.

But he was.

He cried out suddenly, jumping back, urine spraying

his shoes. He moved forward again, a scream rising in his throat.

He was peeing green. Then red. Then green. Christmas colors.

Oh, God, what the hell had been in his drinks! Red again. Blood. Maybe he had something. Maybe he was bleeding . . .

No. Green again. He was peeing Christmas colors. And with each little slosh now . . .

There seemed to be music. Bells. His balls were ringing. Christmas music to go with the Christmas colors. "Jingle Bells." Oh, no. God, no.

He jiggled, stepped forward, hopped up and down. He had to stop.

The flow came to an end, brilliant green and magenta red, twirling together like a frozen yogurt cone.

He staggered back.

Another man entered the john. Jimmy grabbed the fellow's arm. "Have you ever peed in Christmas colors?" Jimmy demanded.

The young fellow didn't answer.

He didn't even pee. He broke free of Jimmy's hold, and hurried out of the john.

Jimmy made it over to the sinks. Whoa, that was a mistake, he thought, as he stared at his reflection, rubbing his chin. Who or what had he expected to see? The James Michael O'Connor of the old days, Harvard grad, a man in impeccable physical shape, intelligence gleaming from his eyes? Women found him exciting; men thought that he was full of power and potential . . .

He needed a shave. Hadn't he bothered that morning? Christmas Eve, he should have been coming home early, should have played with the kids to give Sharon some time to get ready, should have shaved and showered and dressed for dinner. He needed a haircut, too. Maybe even a girdle or a month at a friggin' health spa.

Not that bad, not that bad, he told himself.

But, God, yes . . .

Even as he stared at himself, he was changing.

His cheeks first. They were more than ruddy. "Gin blossoms," filled with ugly broken capillaries and other blood vessels, spread out across his cheeks.

And then . . .

His cheeks were spreading, too. Broadening. And sagging. Oh, man. He was starting to look like a bloodhound. And his eyes . . . the green was brilliant against the red crisscrossing the whites. He was growing more and more haggard looking, his eye sockets deeper.

Then he couldn't see himself clearly anymore. He was being pushed away from the sink and the mirror.

By the size of his gut.

He blinked. Still there.

"Oh, sweet Jesus . . ." he breathed out.

He closed his eyes once again. Okay, okay, he was drinking too much.

Opened his eyes.

He still looked like an old sot who'd been on the sauce

a good fifty years. He needed to go home. Like this? He couldn't go anywhere.

Yes, he could. He could always go home. No matter what. No matter how he looked, no matter how he'd aged. Sharon would always be there. Never condemning. How strange. She was so quiet. She was his rock. She always had been.

He opened his eyes. Oh, God, he had been having hallucinations. His face was back. Almost back. Maybe it never would come back completely. Because you could begin to see the strains of alcohol abuse in it. He wasn't as young as he had been. And there were the faint beginnings of gin blossoms in his cheeks.

He closed his eyes again. His hands started shaking. He needed another drink. That was what he needed. A drink.

He pushed away from the sink. Remembered that red and green stream of Christmas pee and hurried out of the men's room.

Sharon O'Connor stepped onto the porch of her home. Once, it had been open. Then it had been screened. Two winters ago, they had "winterized" it, adding windows over the screens that could still be slid completely open when the spring came. It was a warm room with a round table on which the kids liked to play cards, two chaises, and two wicker chairs. The upholstery was a rough brocade in burgundy and cream flowers; it seemed to suit in both winter and summer. She loved the room. Tonight, though, she'd slipped out here to look anxiously up and down the street. For Jimmy.

She saw a figure huddled beneath a streetlamp. For a moment, she thought it was her husband—hurt, so drunk he couldn't stagger into the house. She went running out to him.

"Jimmy!" she whispered, setting her arms around the shoulders of the figure.

She knew instantly that it wasn't him. These shoulders were frail, the coat was worn—Salvation Army issue.

A face turned to hers. Such an odd face! The eyes so old, so pale a blue, the cheekbones so sunken and narrow.

"My Lord! Are you all right? It's freezing out here!" Sharon exclaimed.

The woman smiled. It was an oddly beautiful smile. "I manage," she said. "Thank you for asking. Thank you for caring."

It was a rough world. Sharon knew it. She also knew that her father would have apoplexy if he knew she was dragging a homeless, possibly infected and infectious stranger into her house.

But she had to do something, and she didn't think a few dollars from the Christmas piggybank would suffice. "Listen, come in—"

"No!"

"Just for a few minutes!" Sharon whispered. She drew her fingers to her lips. "Shh . . . We won't tell anyone. I'll put you on my porch for a few minutes, get you some soup, and a coat. This thing is threadbare.''

"You're kind. Extremely kind. But—"

"Oh, I'm chicken, too. I don't want my father or my husband—if he ever shows up—to know I'm bringing you in."

"Wait, now. You're very kind, but I don't want to cause you trouble—it's Christmas Eve. I can manage, I've been doing so a long time—"

"Come in, just soup and a coat. And yes, it's Christmas Eve and . . ." Sharon paused, shrugged, and smiled. "And this may be the only really Christmasy thing I've done in a very long time. Please, come in."

"I—"

"My name is Sharon O'Connor."

"Margaret. Er, Maggie. Maggie St. Johns."

"Well, Maggie St. Johns, please do come in, warm up for a bit!"

Sharon offered what she hoped was her best, warmest smile. Very uncertain, Maggie allowed her to propel her toward the house.

"Where the hell have you been?" Don demanded as Cathy slid back onto her bar stool at Mulligan's.

She arched her brow to her husband. "Don, I keep warning you, under the circumstances, you've really got to watch the language."

He lifted a hand, frowning, ready to argue with her,

then exhaled, a long breath. "Old habits die hard, what can I say?"

"How did you do?" Cathy asked anxiously.

"I thought I had him," Don said glumly. He pointed across the bar. "I lost him. I was very close. And clever and imaginative, so I thought."

"But . . . ?"

Don lifted his shoulders. "He was ready to run home and sober up—but he decided he needed another drink instead. Where were you?"

"Out finding Maggie St. Johns."

"Oh?"

"I think my first miracle is in process."

"Really?"

"I left Maggie in front of O'Connor's home. With O'Connor's wife."

Don nodded. "If we reappear, do you think I could drink a dark ale? I'd really like to have some one last time."

"Don, we're working on eternity here . . ." Cathy stopped, shrugging. "Let's try it."

They reappeared. It was simple, a thought process. The amount of Christmas cheer in the place was evident when no more than three of the customers even blinked to suddenly see the two of them sitting there.

As Don ordered two dark ales, Cathy realized he was staring at O'Connor all the while.

O'Connor looked at the two of them as he talked to a chum who'd stood by him. He offered Cathy a strange kind of half-smile she had seen before. It was an acknowledgment that she might be intriguing, but she was with someone else. It wasn't a smile she had ever minded—sometimes it meant that the guy smiling was taken as well. She had the feeling O'Connor might be the kind of flirt who enjoyed attention and didn't mind a bit of talk, but who withdrew if the going got serious.

He loved his wife. He just didn't realize how much.

She smiled back at him. And then began playing with the power of suggestion.

She was acquiring a knack for it, she thought.

The woman was pretty. More than that. She was exotic. With a great, come-hither smile. But she was with a guy, one she seemed to know really well. Strange that she should keep looking at him that way, Jimmy thought, when it seemed she was with her old man.

Angela dipped and danced. He looked from the woman down the bar to her.

And almost fell off his bar stool.

It was the woman. Her face. The dark hair, falling around her shoulders as she shimmied and shook and dipped . . .

His eyes flew back across the bar. She was still sitting there with her husband.

The dancer dipped down beside him. Angela. It would be Angela when he looked up . . .

No. The dark-haired beauty.

He closed his eyes. Blinked hard. Oh, God. It was still her. Close to him, smiling. Whispering. "Come out back, Jimmy O'Connor. Come out back now."

CHAPTER 6

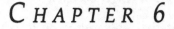

"Just what are you doing?" Don demanded.

"Sipping brown ale. I think I've figured this out. When we're invisible, we can't possibly do such things. The beer would just pour onto the table. When we are visible, we're subject to earthly laws—"

"Cathy, that is not at all what I'm talking about. What are you making him see?"

She grinned. "An Angel."

"A Cathy Angel by any chance? Cathy, just what is it you're doing? Oh-my-God! You've put yourself up there, dancing! Cathy—"

"It's just the power of suggestion!"

"And whose body are you suggesting up there?"

"I'm just trying to get him out of here. And look, he's going. Come on, we have to follow him."

They both stood quickly in the crowded pub. Cathy caught Don's hand, and they weaved through the place together, trying to follow closely behind Jimmy O'Connor.

O'Connor reached the narrow back alleyway of Mulligan's. He stood there baffled, scratching his head. Cathy let go of Don's hand, disappeared and reappeared directly behind Jimmy. She tapped on his shoulder. He let out a startled cry, spinning around. Then he jumped away from her, stared from her to Don.

"Cathy, come on, now, what the hell kind of miracle is it going to be if we give him a heart attack and he dies?"

"What did you say?" Jimmy asked Don. "Who are you people? What do you . . . want?" He stared at Cathy again, swallowed hard.

"What did you do to him?" Don asked Cathy, a fine tinge of jealousy in his voice.

"Nothing that bad, honest!" Cathy protested.

"Who are you? What are you after? Take my wallet, I'll just hand it to you . . ."

"You'd just hand it over. No reflexes—too much booze, huh?" Don said.

"Don't tell him that!" Cathy chided. "There's too much violence these days. He has a wife and little children depending on him. He should never put up a fight if someone tries to steal his wallet"

"Cathy!" Don said with some aggravation. "We're trying to make him see the error of his ways. Look at you!" Don commanded Jimmy. "Within another year, you will have flesh you can't get rid of around your jowls! Within another few years, you could be on the streets, drinking gin while sleeping against a damned dumpster.''

"Watch the 'damned,' Don," Cathy warned.

Jimmy looked from one of them to the other. Groaned, shook his head as if trying to clear his vision, trying to make them disappear.

"He can't go home like that," Cathy said.

"He needs a cup of coffee," Don told her.

"Coming right up. Cream and sugar?" Cathy asked Jimmy.

"I don't want coffee."

"Black. Black coffee," Don told Cathy.

Jimmy looked down. Suddenly there was a Styrofoam cup of steaming dark liquid in his hands. He screamed. Threw the cup away from himself. Hot coffee flew everywhere, luckily missing his clothing and skin.

"He needs another cup," Don said.

"Now don't lose this one. I'm not good at all at this stuff yet," Cathy warned.

Another cup appeared in Jimmy's hands. He held on to it, his hands shaking violently.

"Come on, now, have a sip," Cathy urged.

Jimmy O'Connor sipped his coffee, staring at them. "I've gone to hell!" he whispered, and sipped the coffee.

"Not yet, but you might well have been headed there," Cathy told him.

Jimmy took a look at her. Drank the rest of the coffee in one swallow.

"Think he's ready to go home?" Don asked Cathy.

"Sure."

"Where's his car?"

Jimmy O'Connor's eyes darted toward a smart-looking little Mazda. The Mazda's lights blinked on; its engine revved. A second later, the Mazda leapt toward them.

"No," Jimmy O'Connor said. "No, no, no . . ."

He shook his head, stared at his car, dropped the coffee cup, and started running toward the street.

"Truck!" Cathy cried out.

Jimmy O'Connor didn't hear her. He raced out onto the road, then stood dead still in the center of it, mesmerized by the lights.

Don came flying out, slamming into Jimmy, hurtling them both to the side of the road as the vehicle sped on by.

"Hey!" Cathy shrieked after the truck, but it was gone, heading into the night. Cathy ran over to where both men lay on their backs, side by side now. She dropped to one knee beside them. Don groaned. Jimmy just stared up at her.

"Don, are you . . . hurt?"

He groaned. "The brown ale was good. The truck was bad," he said. Cathy helped him up. In turn, he stretched a hand down to Jimmy O'Connor.

Jimmy came to his feet, staring at them both. "I saw my life," he said. "Saw those lights, then my life. And I wanted to live. To go home. To Sharon. My kids. I have the world's greatest son, the prettiest daughter. My in-laws . . ." He shrugged.

"Hey, you know a little schism with the in-laws is natural," Don said.

"It is?" Cathy demanded.

"A tiny schism," Don said.

"I just always thought that Sharon—she was always there—that she should be, that she'd always be. And I didn't really realize just what that meant. I have to get home, I have to—" He broke off, staring at Cathy. "Can you do more of that coffee thing?" He started patting his coat pockets. "I need a comb. I need—"

"Coffee," Cathy told him.

"Comb." Don produced one.

Jimmy drank another cup of coffee. Accepted the comb, pulled it through his hair.

"How do I look?"

"You'll do," Cathy told him.

He grinned at her suddenly, glanced at Don wryly. "She does nicely, too."

"Yeah?" Don arched a brow to his wife.

"Who are you two? What are you?" Jimmy demanded.

"The Angels," Don said.

"Cathy and Don Angel," Cathy said firmly, staring at her husband.

"But what—" Jimmy began.

"Does it matter who or what we are?" Don asked him quietly.

Jimmy shook his head. "Not if . . . not if you'll pretend to be clients for me—for a little bit. Please. Give me an excuse for being so late tonight. I swear to you, I'll never need another one."

"I'll get the car," Don said.

"I'll drive!" Jimmy insisted.

"I'll get the car," Cathy said.

The Mazda's lights blazed; the car came forward, just like an obedient puppy. The three of them piled into it. Before Jimmy could touch the wheel, the Mazda jerked into action, taking them the few blocks home to Jimmy O'Connor's house.

As Jimmy got out of the car and stared at the place, Cathy and Don got out to stand behind him.

"I'm suddenly afraid to go home," Jimmy said. He'd come home, yeah, but he was late. Sharon would forgive him; she'd try to make everything appear all right in front of her parents. Still, he felt guilty. Oh, God, he thought, just give me this one chance without words being said, without the kids being hurt. Please, I just need one more chance . . .

"Why are you afraid?" Don demanded.

Jimmy shook his head. "I don't exactly know except that maybe . . . I didn't know before what I've come so close to losing."

Don took him by the arm. Firmly, Jimmy thought. "Let's go," Don insisted.

"Hey, slow down. My in-laws are in there."

"But we haven't got all night," Don said firmly.

Cathy caught Jimmy's other arm. Between them, they managed to lead him up the steps and into the house before he could protest again.

"Okay, okay," Jimmy said. He fumbled for his key. Before he could find it, the front door flew open. A little boy with bright, hopeful eyes stood there. "Daddy?"

"Hey, squirt, I'm home," Jimmy said, plucking up his son. He stepped into the house, followed by Cathy and Don. "Where's your mom?" he asked.

"In the kitchen," the little boy said.

"Ah, Mum, Dad," Jimmy said, coming into the living room. He was still awkward, uncertain. Cathy and Don followed closely behind him. Cathy stepped forward to greet the handsome older couple who had come to check out the commotion at the front door. "Cathy and Don, I'd like you to meet my in-laws, Abby and Earl Challifour. Abby, Earl . . . Cathy and Don Angel."

"How do you do?" Earl Challifour said politely, shaking their hands. He looked at his son-in-law curiously, but seemed satisfied that Jimmy O'Connor was sober.

"And of course," Jimmy continued, "I'd like you to meet my son Timmy, and over there . . ." Jimmy hesitated a minute, "Laura, come over here sweetie. Meet Mr. and Mrs. Angel."

Laura, looking pretty in her little velvet pinafore, came shyly forward. She went straight to Cathy, smiling. "Are you really an angel?" she asked.

Cathy stooped down to her. "I really am—I have been

since I married Don. It's his last name. So it's been mine since we married. Your mommy took your daddy's name, O'Connor. Like your own."

"Oh," Laura said. "You look like an angel."

"Sweetheart, angels have wings!" Abby Challifour said, shaking her head to Cathy in a manner that said Kids! without hurting little Laura's feelings.

"You have to be a real angel," Laura insisted.

"Laura!" her grandmother murmured. "I am so sorry—"

"No, no, we're sorry," Don broke in. "We didn't mean to keep Jimmy working so late, it's just that we're going to be hit with a big problem if all our plans aren't solidified by the new year."

"Your plans?" Abby Challifour said with polite enthusiasm.

"For our new house," Cathy said.

"For the business—" Don began.

"The business," Cathy said.

"House—" Don began.

He laughed. "We're just trying to have everything done," he said to the Challifours.

"Mum, Dad, excuse us, will you? I want Cathy and Don to meet Sharon."

"Yes, please," Cathy said, and she hurried along with Jimmy O'Connor into the kitchen. Jimmy entered, calling out his wife's name.

They could see Sharon out on the pretty little enclosed side porch. Jimmy stepped on out to talk to her.

"Jimmy!" She was startled to see him in the house. He looked at Sharon, into her eyes—velvet brown, soft, warm, giving—she smiled. A beautiful smile. Other than the roundness of her stomach, she remained slim. Her short brown hair was stylishly cut. And when she smiled, when her eyes touched Jimmy's, she wasn't just pretty, she was beautiful.

He took her into his arms and kissed her soundly. "I love you," he whispered.

"Jimmy . . . I'm so glad that you're home. I was so afraid that—"

She broke off because he kissed her. Kissed her lips, her forehead, her cheeks, her lips.

"I almost didn't come home," he said very quickly. "I—I didn't know that I wanted to be home, that I needed to be home. I love you so much, I—"

He broke off, looking over his wife's shoulder and suddenly realizing that there was a bag lady sitting at the table on his porch.

"Who . . . who . . . ?"

"This is, er, Maggie," Sharon said uneasily. "Everybody needs a little warmth at Christmas," they both heard.

Cathy Angel was standing in the doorway to the porch.

Sharon looked at Jimmy.

"Who . . . er . . . ?"

"Cathy, my wife, Sharon. Sharon, Cathy Angel. And Don—that's her husband right behind her."

"Hello," Sharon said.

"Merry Christmas," Cathy said.

"Thanks." Sharon stared at them, then smiled suddenly, her insight much like her daughter's. "Thank you, really. You brought Jimmy home tonight, didn't you?"

"He really did want to be here," Don said.

"Okay, but now who—" Jimmy began again.

"Maggie. This is Maggie St. Johns," Sharon said.

"Hi, Maggie."

"I can just leave—" Maggie began.

"No!" Jimmy, Sharon, Don, and Cathy said in unison.

"You're welcome here, honest to God, you're welcome," Jimmy said to her. "Just sit tight for a minute, huh, Maggie? Promise me. Sharon, you come into the kitchen with me for just a second." He smiled at Maggie, urging Sharon toward the kitchen. He propelled her into it, right behind Cathy and Don, holding her hand tightly.

Sharon smiled at her unexpected guests a little awkwardly. "Can I get you something?" she offered.

"No," Jimmy told her. "Sharon—"

"Jimmy, that's so rude."

"Sharon, they brought me home. Trust me, they don't want anything. I just want a minute with you." He stared at Cathy and Don. "You know, it would definitely be a minor miracle if my father-in-law were to allow me a few more minutes alone with my wife. Perhaps, if the two of you were to talk with him and Mum for a bit, it would give me a chance . . .''

"Is that on our list?" Don said to Cathy.

"You are pushing it, don't you think?" she replied.

"What list?" Sharon asked.

"Never mind. Jimmy, we'll go in and have a conversation with your in-laws and keep them busy for a bit. You two . . . enjoy," Don said. He took Cathy's arm and led her into the parlor. "I guess he could be a grumpy old fellow, Sharon's dad, eh?" Don said. "Reminds me of your father, Cathy."

Cathy kicked him discreetly on the shin.

Then they went into the parlor. From the kitchen, Jimmy and Sharon could hear them beginning a conversation with Sharon's parents.

Sharon looked up at Jimmy, her arms locked around his neck.

"Who are they?" she queried. Her eyes were shining. There had been tears in them, Jimmy realized. She was smiling against that beautiful, soft glitter in her eyes.

"I told you, sweetheart, Cathy and Don. The Angels."

"Angels?"

"Their last name is Angel. Cathy and Don Angel."

"They aren't clients."

"No. They aren't clients."

"Then who—"

"I don't want to know. I don't even want to ask."

She shook her head. "They are angels. They brought you home to me."

He enveloped her in his arms. "I'm home forever, I promise it, every single night. I won't stray, and I won't fall."

"Jimmy—"

"I promise it."

"If you falter, I'll be here."

"You've been a damned angel," he told her.

"I love you so very much."

"That's a damned miracle," he told her.

He kissed his wife, very tenderly. Took her hand. "Let's go see the kids and the gorgons."

"Jimmy!"

"Let's go see the kids and my wonderful in-laws."

She arched a brow and started to laugh. Jimmy O'Connor began to leave the kitchen, then remembered the poor skinny creature sipping soup on his back porch.

"Sharon, have you got anything that wretched creature could wear besides that old coat you've put over her?"

"Of course."

"She's skin and bones."

"I make clothing, remember."

"I didn't mean you had to give her something brand new."

Sharon smiled. "I just happen to have something brand new. I'll be right back."

Twenty minutes later, their guest was washed and dressed in new stockings, a wool, knit dress, and an embroidered sweater. Her shoes were still a little off; but her hair had cleaned up beautifully. Before the shower, she'd looked like a very old woman, now it was clear she was only in her late thirties or early forties. She was as grateful as she was stunned.

"You're going to have Christmas with us," Jimmy told her.

"Oh, I can't. I can't possibly."

"Why not?" Jimmy demanded.

"It just wouldn't be right. I couldn't impose."

"You're not imposing," Sharon said firmly, but she looked back to her husband, "How do we explain her to my folks?"

"Your name is Maggie, right?" Jimmy said to the woman.

She nodded.

Jimmy shrugged. "She's my cousin, Maggie, just in from the city."

"Can there possibly be a stray O'Connor cousin?"

"Distant cousin, then."

"From what city?" Sharon asked.

"Who cares? Pick a city."

"New York?" Maggie suggested happily. "I always liked New York."

"Sure. Come along now, Cousin Maggie."

They started into the parlor. Jimmy hung back just a shade, then grabbed his wife and kissed her once again, a wet, sloppy kiss filled with awkward gratitude, promise, and love.

"Merry Christmas," he told her.

She smiled.

"God, yes. Merry Christmas."

They joined her folks, the kids, the Angels. Maggie was wonderful with children. She might well have been a cousin, she was so quick and loving with them.

The O'Connor house was filled with warmth. With laughter, with a friendly flow of conversation.

With Christmas magic.

"We may need help with the new baby, you know," Jimmy said to Sharon at one point. She was carving the turkey which, miraculously, appeared to be not just edible but delicious.

Maggie was seated on the floor out in the parlor, playing an alphabet game with Laura.

"She could be perfect," Sharon agreed.

"We can try it."

"We have the apartment over the garage."

"Perfect. Oh, Jimmy, that will be just perfect, if we can give her a chance!"

No one knew quite when the Angels left. Suddenly they were there, suddenly they weren't.

And it wasn't until the next day, until Jimmy and Sharon read their names in conjunction with the terrible accident just outside of New York City, that the family realized they couldn't have been there at all.

CHAPTER 7

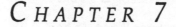

"Perhaps the most amazing thing about beliefs is that no matter how widely they differ, similarities can be found. Though the ancient gods and goddesses of, say, the Greeks, Romans, and Norsemen have little bearing upon the religions of Christians, Muslims, Jews, and Zoroastrians, in all these beliefs are certain creatures who carry out quite similar tasks."

The woman speaking was young, at twenty-seven not much older than the students who had gathered to listen to her speak on Christmas Eve. She was a favorite within the university, admired for her many sterling qualities, and for her looks as well, though knowledge of her past kept any lustful students at bay. She had rich auburn hair worn in a soft swing-style to her shoulders, lime green eyes, beautiful classical features, and though she was small, not a hair over five-foot-two, she was very nicely put together, and, as one of her male students was fond of saying behind her back, good things, surely very good things, came in small packages.

"The Valkyries of the Norsemen watch them upon the battlefield, ready to sweep up the soul of a fierce and brave warrior and take him to Valhalla," she continued. "Mercury is a messenger, as is Mars. In our modern, civilized society, we tend to look back on such beliefs as fairy tales, forgetting that Christianity, indeed, the New Testament, offers us new insights into tales told in ancient times as well. What we know about angels originates not so much in the Bible as we may read it today, but in books outside the realm of what we now accept as orthodox scriptures and canons of our religions. Much of our information comes from the three great Chronicles of Enoch, which were set together from much older sources. Enoch was known to be a truth-speaker; nonetheless, St. Jerome declared his chronicles to be apocryphal in the fourth century A.D. Despite that, they make wonderful stories, giving us endless images of ten separate heavens in which angels may be punished for various acts of disobedience. The Old Testament mentions only three angels by name, and the Catholic Book of Tobit is included. In the New Testament, we have a Magnificent Seven—a divine grouping of archangels, with only four names being consistently mentioned: Michael, Gabriel, Rafael, and Uriel. One very intriguing thought is that the ancient word '*el*' in Sumerian, meaning brightness of shining, coincides with very similar-sounding words in other languages—such as 'elf' in

English, meaning shining being. Micha-el translates into the phrase 'who is as God.' According to tradition and lore, Michael is the greatest of the archangels. He appeared to Moses in the midst of a burning bush, he is said to have stayed the hand of Abraham before he would have slain his own son in God's glory. Michael is a warrior, who single-handedly and overnight wiped out nearly two hundred thousand men from the army of an Assyrian king who was threatening Jerusalem. He is most certainly the hero of that first war against the fallen angel, Satan."

"It might have been nice to have met Michael," Don murmured to Cathy.

"Maybe that's coming at a later date," she suggested. Maybe . . .

The alternatives to a return upward were quite grim.

For the present, they had found themselves seated halfway up in the auditorium, listening, watching.

"Think Gabriel sent us here for an education?" Cathy asked.

Don grunted. "It will depend on just how much this young woman raves about Gabriel, don't you think?"

"Don—"

"I'll be nice, Cathy. Read the list, please. I'm not quite certain what this young lady's great trouble can be."

"She is very attractive," Cathy murmured, but then she whispered a soft, "Oh!"

"What?"

"This is so sad!"

"Tell me."

"She was married and had a baby. There were complications in labor, the cord got wrapped around the baby's neck. The baby was born retarded, and apparently her husband couldn't deal with the situation. They had words, and he wound up leaving her. But she adored her little boy, anyway, and she was more or less getting along okay, then . . ."

"Then?"

"She was with her son and her parents last year in a commuter plane on the way to a specialist, and"—Cathy hesitated, shaking her head—"the plane crashed. Her folks and little boy were killed. And she was blinded."

"She's blind!" Michael said, startled, looking at the beautiful young woman who was speaking.

"Legally. She can see shadows—fuzz—some forms. Her retinas were damaged."

"Surgery could solve that . . . couldn't it?"

"She needs a donor."

"Are we supposed to find one?" Don asked, praying that they were not. He had ghastly visions of himself and Cathy digging up graveyards to find living eyes. Béla Lugosi, Vincent Price, Peter Lorre—all flashed through his mind in ghoulish roles as grave robbers.

"Cathy? Please tell me we're not supposed to find eyes for her!"

She shook her head. "We're not."

"What are we supposed to do for her then?"

She looked at him. "Keep her from committing suicide," she said.

"Oh, God. Your miracle or mine?"

"Mine," Cathy whispered.

"How could mine possibly be worse?"

Cathy shrugged.

"Well?"

"Well, what?"

"What's my miracle? Considering Gabriel likes you and doesn't like me, mine is sure to be a real winner if it's going to be harder than yours."

"It's really not such a hard task."

"Well, tell me!"

"There's a nun near here, living in a home for members of her order who have retired from active service."

"And?"

"She's dying."

"Great. Of what?"

"Cancer and other complications."

He groaned. "Can there be a miracle cure? Am I supposed to make her better?"

"No."

"Then?"

"She's afraid."

"A nun—afraid to die?"

"She's been a bit blind-sided as well, it seems. Whatever, she's afraid."

"She's smart."

"You have to make death easy for her."

He groaned softly. There was a catch to everything, it seemed. Don't cure her—just make it easy for her to die. Easy to say.

But one miracle at a time, he told himself. They were assigned separate ones, but they worked as a couple. A team.

And they were striving to remain a team while the hours and minutes of Christmas Eve ticked away.

They were here with Rowenna Trent right now. The young woman with the beautiful face.

"I guess we start with Rowenna," Don murmured.

"How incredibly sad," Cathy whispered. "It seems she was blinded to her faith as well."

Rowenna Trent didn't appear to be blind in any way. She had a beautiful smile, and her gaze wasn't at all vacant. She seemed to see—shadows, fuzz, Cathy had said—as she addressed the audience, talking in a crystal-clear, well-modulated voice.

"After Michael, we have Gabriel. Gabriel rules the cherubim—Eden, as well, and the first heaven. He is known to be the angel of Truth, Annunciation, Resurrection, Mercy, Revelation—and Death. The angels, in general, are supposed to be very close to mankind, to bring God's word to man. As ruler of the first heaven, Gabriel is necessarily very close to man. And by the way, a number of schools of thought suggest that Gabriel might be the only woman among the very high echelon of heaven."

Rowenna Trent stopped speaking, smiling as her students giggled, the girls teasing the boys.

"Hmmph!" Don snorted. "I could assure them that Mister-Gabriel-in-his-Versace likes women much more than men!"

"Shush," Cathy said.

Rowenna Trent cocked her head slightly, feeling the strangest little tremor shoot down her spine. She'd heard an odd whispering. She stared out over her audience, but that didn't help. The people she was addressing remained vague and shadowy. Shapes, shades, and nothing more. And yet she sensed . . .

"Miss Trent!" She recognized the voice. Rocky Morris, a great hulk on the university's formidable football team.

"Yes, Rocky?" She saw a shadow rise and knew that he had stood to address her.

"There are many, you know, who say that angels absolutely can't be females."

"Ah, yes, Rocky. Gabri-el is assumed to have come from the Sumerian root *gbr, gabri,* meaning *gubernator* or governor. But for those doubting Thomases who need to believe in male superiority, the word can also mean 'Divine Husband.' Gabriel did bring word to Mary about the birth of Christ—God's message to his handmaiden."

"Well, it's only logical, isn't it?" Rocky asked. Big, young, cocky, with longish sandy hair despite the discomfort it must cause him in a helmet, he was determined to go on. "Women have been put in their places in both the Old Testament and the New Testament. Isn't it true that Lilith, who was the first wife of Adam, was cast down to become the bride of Satan partially because she wanted to . . . er, you know . . . be on top— when she was supposed to be in a subordinate position on the bottom? Would that mean God still gets mad at babes who want the, er, superior position?"

Rowenna heard a loudly audible sniff, and knew that the next speaker was Jill, his wife, a hardworking law student who was expecting a baby in the spring. "God would forgive me, I know, Rocky, because you're two hundred and forty pounds of sheer agony at this point!"

Laughter arose in the auditorium, and Rowenna smiled toward Jill. She had to admit, she enjoyed these sessions at the campus parish center. It was Christmas Eve, but a number of the kids—kids! they were young adults!—hadn't been able to go home, or they made their homes here, so when she gave this Christmas Eve lecture on angels, many more had come than she had ever expected. They certainly weren't required to be here this evening.

"You are all going to have to take up your sexual habits with the Almighty on your own," she told them, running her fingers over the Braille book she had brought to refresh her memory on the history and myths of angels. She taught ancient history and theology, and though she had lost much of her enthusiasm during the last year, she still did a lot of work at the parish student center—dragged into activities by her cousin who was a young priest at the campus church. William tried so hard on her behalf. But he couldn't help.

Her students did. Sometimes. But not enough. Not enough to wash away the pain that so constantly circled around her. She'd been in the hospital last year. Trying to understand that her parents were dead. That Jeremy was dead. Just two years old, so trusting, so sweet, gone forever. Gone into God's embrace, William had tried to assure her. But she couldn't accept that. Joshua had turned against her and Jeremy; maybe God had done the same. Maybe she had protested what God had done to her, and because of that, He had turned away from her and everyone associated with her. She'd come back to work because of William, she'd tried because of William, but now it was Christmas Eve again, and she didn't think that she could bear the pain. There was no one to care anymore. The kids, her students, were great; but they had their own lives. And William had his faith, his calling—he would go on. Joshua had come back, but too late . . .

Joshua. She could still remember her ex-husband at her bedside in the hospital outside Pittsburgh. Holding her hand. She had touched his face, and felt his tears. But she couldn't forgive him.

And she couldn't forgive herself.

Maybe that was the worst of it. She couldn't forgive herself. For living, when Jeremy and her parents had died.

She didn't want to face the memories now. She didn't want to let her students go. She had to.

But, oh . . .

She didn't want to be alone tonight.

To have to face life or death on her own.

She had been arguing with herself for days now. She knew the cruelty of the act to others, but those who loved her most were gone. Her mother, her father, her baby . . .

It was wrong. So wrong . . .

She was sinking nonetheless. And no one knew, she prayed. She wouldn't purposely draw anyone else in the world into this pain, not her best friend, not her worst enemy.

Angels . . . she reminded herself.

Tonight, she might see them.

Or face damnation.

"Rafa-el! He is the ruler of the Second Heaven and is the 'healer' angel. He is one of the seven angels of the throne, by his own admission—as he says himself in the Book of Tobit. Let's see, he guards the Tree of Life in Eden, and he is ruler of the Order of Virtues. A very important angel, he is often associated with the serpent or snake, a symbol for . . . ?"

"Doctors!" A student called out cheerfully.

"Exactly."

"Rafael is said to heal men; he is the angel of the sun, and is therefore considered to have a special disposition; he is friendly, quick to laugh. In the Tobit, he walks with Tobias, commands him to catch a big fish, then tells him what healing qualities the pieces and organs of the fish can offer. But he is also a guide of the underworld, or 'Pit' in Hebrew, and it is said that he can appear in monstrous forms. After Rafael, we have Uri-el—'Fire of God.' And can he be fiery! He is the angel who will bring forth order, and in that command, Uriel can be merciless, quite brutal. Those who do not find redemption will burn in everlasting fire. Uriel will see to it that they are punished eternally."

"Want to say something about him, Rocky?" a classmate called out teasingly.

"Nope. I don't think I want to mess with old Uri-el!" Rocky called back cheerfully. "Any more angels tonight, Miss Trent?"

Rowenna bit lightly into her lower lip. She closed the Braille reference book she had before her, shaking her head.

It was Christmas Eve.

Agony to her.

A celebration to others.

She had to let her students go.

"Just the angels on your shoulders!" she told them lightly. "Good night, Merry Christmas to all of you."

"Merry Christmas!" came back to her in a soft chorus. The students began to file out of the student-center auditorium. Jill stepped to the podium.

"Rowenna, Rocky and I would like to invite you to

come home with us for a while. Maybe even spend the night. Wake up Christmas morning with . . . us."

Rowenna smiled at Jill. She shook her head. "Thank you. I have plans."

"Really? You won't be alone?"

"I won't be," Rowenna lied. "Get that lug of yours home and enjoy Christmas Eve. It's the last one the two of you will have alone. That baby is a blessing, of course, but the little sweethearts do change your life."

"Rowenna, really, Rocky and I have lots of time together. I wish you'd come with us."

"I'm fine. I do have plans, and you young people need to get on home and enjoy one another."

"But—"

"Go!" Rowenna said firmly.

"Maybe you'll stop by tomorrow?" Rocky suggested.

"Sure," Rowenna lied. She wasn't going to be here tomorrow. She hoped they wouldn't be hurt too badly by what she meant to do, but she couldn't bear the pain any longer. She couldn't see, but it was easy to remember the Christmas carols coming over the plane's speakers right before the engines had failed, before she had fallen from the sky into this pit of darkness . . .

"Tomorrow, then!" Rocky insisted. "Can we see you out?"

She shook her head. "I have my cane, and I'm practically across the street," she assured them.

When the last of her students had trailed out, she collected her handbag, books, and cane. She knew the way

in and out of the small auditorium. From there, she just
had to go across the street, around the corner, and down
a few houses. She had learned a great deal in a year.
Braille—that had come easily enough. Listening—that
had come harder. But now, she heard little things. A car
coming from a long way off. A dog barking a street
away. Footsteps moving slowly behind her. Whispering.

Was she about to be attacked? Murdered for her
handbag. She slowed her gait.

Come! Come slice through this life of shadow! I told
Joshua that Jeremy could not go to a home, that I would
be with him. That my mom would be with him while I
taught my classes, that I didn't mind sacrificing our
lives for our son.

Our lives. She had to admit, she hadn't listened to a
word Joshua had said to her. She had hated him, had
been furious that he hadn't understood her need to be
near the boy at all times. She could not abandon her son
to others. She had created him.

Rowenna stopped walking. She no longer heard the
footsteps behind her. The only whisper was that of the
soft wind. Christmas Eve in South Florida. No snow,
and this year, the temperature was a balmy seventy-five
degrees.

She tapped along the walkway to the pretty little
house she had rented in the community of Coral Gables.
She was blinded to it now, but she could still see it in her
mind's eye. Three bedrooms, kitchen, living room, fam-

ily room, screened porch with a small but adequate fifteen-by-thirty-foot swimming pool. It would have been perfect for Jeremy. She had meant to make sure that he had the constant therapy of water exercises.

Her bedroom, once *their* bedroom. Joshua had lived with her here for a while. Until it had been too much. Until he had left his own teaching position. He'd sent money. She'd never cashed his checks. She hadn't talked to him until he had come to the hospital; then she had begged him to go away, and he finally had.

It was ironic. He had buried Jeremy and her parents. She had still been unconscious, in critical condition, when they had all been laid to rest.

I want to die, she told herself.

Hundreds of murders in Dade County yearly. And no one would come for her.

Accidents. Dozens a day.

She lived on.

Christmas Eve.

Too painful to be borne.

She turned the handle of her door. She never locked it. Ironically enough, she'd never been robbed.

She entered the house, dropped her books and handbag on the small table just inside the doorway. The master bedroom lay to her far left; the other two were down the hall to the right. Living room before her; family room and kitchen behind that.

The pool. She could walk into the pool. No, she was

too good a swimmer. She'd never be able to force herself to drown.

There was only one way.

She moved on into the house, only having to feel her way once in the hallway. Jeremy's room, untouched since his death. was now on her left.

To her right was her office. Filled with memorabilia, *things*, that had once made her happy. A giant poster of the Sphinx was up against the wall. Joshua had taken her to Egypt for her twenty-first birthday. They were newly married then; college students themselves. He had saved forever, starved at lunch, to pay for their tickets and accommodations. They'd eaten fruit—beans—and kushari—a mixture of rice, beans, and pasta the entire trip. It had been absolutely worth it. Her little brass figure of the Norse god Wodin sat atop the desk, along with her wooden replica of Zeus. Besides the poster of the Sphinx, her wall was covered with prints. Cheap prints, but still beautifully matted, copies of some of her favorite art, such as *Tobias and the Angels*, fifteenth century, Botticini. *Satan Contemplates the Fall*, Gustave Doré. She couldn't see them anymore, but could picture them in her mind. She had loved myth and religion and philosophy, had been brought up in the Catholic Church and still loved it, especially William's church, but in her studies she had determined that so much was similar among peoples, God simply had shown himself to man in different ways. She had once believed in heaven, in angels, and in hell.

Suicides went to hell . . .

She didn't know what she believed in anymore. Because if there had really been a God, he wouldn't have hurt Jeremy the way He did; He wouldn't have killed her parents along with her son. He wouldn't have left her alive, blinded to everything but pain . . .

"Don't worry, she isn't going to do it yet."

Startled by the sound of whispering, Rowenna spun around. "Who's there?" she demanded.

Nothing. She stood still and listened.

She had learned to listen.

Still nothing. Her imagination.

She sat down behind the desk. Started to open the desk drawer.

Then . . .

The whispering again.

"How do you know?" A woman's voice.

"She hasn't had a last cigarette."

"Maybe she doesn't smoke."

"A last drink then. Cup of tea. I mean, you must do a last *something*, right?"

"Maybe."

"Who is it? Who's there?" Rowenna called out. Again, nothing. No reply. Wonderful. On top of everything else, she was losing her mind. Because suicides went to hell.

Straight to hell. It was a sin. A terrible sin. It was a sin against God, against herself, against her fellow man. It was the most incredibly cruel thing a person could do to her loved ones . . .

Her loved ones were gone.

Not all of them.

She would be damned . . .

No. No one really believed that anymore. The world understood the pain of a suicide these days.

But did God?

She ignored her own voice, wondered if the whispering wasn't a product of her own conscience.

She bit gently into her lower lip, then opened the top drawer. She didn't attempt to look downward. She couldn't see anything at all in the darkened house.

Only shadows.

And darkness.

Haunting, lonely, darkness.

She didn't need to see. She drew out the hefty Magnum there. She was a scholar. Well read. And she'd read about suicide. Pills might just make her sick—if she could find a druggist who'd give her enough of the guaranteed-dead kind.

No. This was the way she chose.

All she had to do was put the gun in her mouth and squeeze the trigger. It would be fast—and foolproof.

Rowenna felt the cold steel. Lifted the gun. Set it into her mouth. Choked, but didn't withdraw it. She moved her fingers against the trigger . . .

And froze.

To her amazement, there were . . .

Voices.

"I thought you said she wasn't going to do it now?"

"Well, I'm sorry. I was wrong. Who'd have imagined she'd be in such a hurry?"

"She *is* suicidal, remember?" An angry hiss.

"But even then—" A husky, masculine whisper.

"We can't argue! What now?" The female voice again, aggravated, anxious.

I am losing my mind! Rowenna thought. First she had lost everything she'd lived for, then her sight. Now she was definitely losing her mind as well.

Squeeze the trigger! she commanded herself. *It's easy, just squeeze . . .*

"No! Don't you dare. Drop that!" she suddenly heard. No longer a whisper. Words. Shouted. Angry, threatening.

The gun was slapped from her. Her finger caught in the trigger.

She heard the explosion . . .

Then dimly . . .

So dimly . . .

Words, again.

Curses!

"Oh, dammit to hell! Now I've gone and done it!"

"Don, your language!"

"What difference does it make now? I think I've managed to kill her myself!"

CHAPTER 8

S ister Mary Claire could feel Death.
It was coming.

And she was terrified.

Horrified. All of her life, she had felt her calling. Had known that she was meant to endure mosquito bites, bee stings, cold nights, hot days, and long, endless hours. She had taken her greatest pleasure in helping little children lost in the world, and it hadn't mattered where. She had enjoyed the time she had taken to raise her own nephew because she had always believed she had time. Time to be with children. Who were young. Who were life. She had always believed . . .

Even when the cancer had come. Even when she had been in pain. Pain was a part of life. She had believed in her Heavenly Father, and she had known that everything would be all right. She had been cheerful through every moment of her illness.

Until now.

Now there was no pain. Now there was morphine. Father William was at her side. He had given her the last rites, and she had managed to listen, but she had wanted to scream, wanted to shout out that it was all a hoax, that words didn't matter, that the Church didn't matter. She was Sister Mary Claire. She was supposed to be so good—a candidate for sainthood, just about. Her endless, never-questioning faith inspired those around her. Her patience, fortitude, and good cheer . . .

It was a lie.

That was what was so horrible! It was as if her whole life had been a lie, a pretense. She had thought she had believed—when there had been nothing. All of her life she had said that she believed.

But she hadn't been dying then.

And now . . .

Now she was.

And she didn't believe.

It had all been a lie. Her whole life. Like millions of others out there, she had just been paying lip service to a fantasy.

Once, there had been life and magic.

Now, there was just death.

She was in her room at the home. Father William— that little puppy, too young to have learned much about the way of the world!—was at her side. It was a spacious enough room. She lived in a wonderfully generous community, and thought, by the very nature of their lives, retired religious did not need much in the way of material luxuries, her surroundings were pleasant. A beautiful painting of Christ beamed down at her. Christ with blond hair and blue eyes, very Anglo, though even now, Mary Claire was convinced that Christ, when he had come to earth, born to Mary, must have been very dark, and in that darkness, far more beautiful—with deep, soulful eyes—than he had ever been portrayed by gentile artists.

Well, she was about to find out. Find out if he was the Son of Man, God's gift to the world. Find out if there was a God, if there was a heaven, an afterlife, a power . . .

Panic seized her. How had she failed to believe? How strange death could be! She lay here now, with no strength in her arms. She could see, but could scarcely move her head. Oh, yes, she could see! The painting of Christ, the intravenous bottle that dripped morphine into her bloodstream—oh, why wouldn't that damned morphine kick in, knock her out cold, let her escape this agony of fear? She wanted to ask for more; she couldn't quite manage to do so. She wanted death to come quickly at one second, fought it the next. Each minute, each second, was agony.

So slow . . .

She looked across the room to where Father William sat, so dear a man, so deeply engrossed in prayer. He prayed for her so studiously, so intently. Poor man, poor foolish man! He prayed for a woman who had suddenly lost all faith, all belief . . .

Because though she had changed, she hadn't changed. She could see her own image in the silver-plated water pitcher at her side, a gift from her nephew when she had come here. She was crinkled, wrinkled, and old.

But not inside! Inside, she was young. No wrinkles marred her face. She was the energetic little woman with the beautiful smile and dazzling eyes who had galvanized summer corps of CCD students into work forces in the worst jungles of Mexico and South America. She had fought the sin of vanity once she had actually taken her vows, because even into her later forties and fifties, she had been a handsome woman. But it wasn't her beauty she remembered now; it was her energy. It remained in her soul. She wondered fervently why God—if He did exist—had allowed people to age so pathetically on the outside, while they never seemed to realize it inside, never saw themselves in the mind's eye as the pathetic, dried-up, and worthless beings they had become?

Because there was no God!

Had there been a God, little children, in wretched villages with no running water, wouldn't have died as skin and bone corpses with big bloated bellies. She wouldn't have seen so many little ones maimed—armless, legless, footless—blown to bits. They looked back at her as she tried to help them, silently begging to know *why?*

Before, she'd had the answers. *God's will.* Rewards for suffering came in heaven, and God welcomed His children as His little lambs; they would find welcome, peace, freedom from pain.

Freedom from pain.

She would be free . . .

She didn't want to die.

She was terrified of dying . . .

She would do anything in the world to stop death. Whether she closed or opened her eyes, she could see too clearly. How damned funny. Just about everything on her had rotted. But she had fantastic vision. Eyes opened, eyes closed.

Eyes opened, she saw the truth. She was a pathetic old woman used up and useless and dying.

Eyes closed. The wrinkles were gone. She was young inside. And beautiful still. And she could not die, could not die . . .

Terror seized her. Filled limbs that should have been numb with death.

She was so afraid she wanted to cry out. To scream. To reach for a hand to hold. To shout and deny what was happening. To cry and blubber and shriek out that she was afraid. If she could only believe again, enough to pray. She didn't want to ruin the pride and grace of her life with such a cowardly demise. If only . . .

She started suddenly, eyes opened as she looked around the room.

She'd heard a voice. Not Father William's well-known tones. A different pitch. One she didn't know.

Mary, I am coming!

There was no one with her. No one at all.

She wasn't just dying. She was losing her mind.

She began to curse the God she didn't believe in anymore. She tried to tell herself that it would be all right. She did have family. George would come to be with her. And maybe Scottie. She loved Scottie so much. If he were to come, and hold her hand . . .

Scottie wouldn't come.

But George would. She wouldn't be so alone. So—

So terrified.

She wouldn't hear voices then.

No, she wouldn't hear them for long.

Death was rushing upon her with the speed of a roller coaster. And she was on a downhill ride, shrieking silently into the night.

Rowenna's head was spinning. She hadn't been shot, which she had thought at first, and to her amazement, her heart was beating a thousand miles an hour in relief. She'd been hit on the head by some kind of a projectile, though, she realized, fumbling around the floor where she had fallen when her desk chair had catapulted backward. Her fingers closed around her image of the god Wodin. The bullet that had discharged from her gun had hit the figure; the figure had hit her head. Amazingly, both were only knicked now.

But she wasn't alone, and she knew it.

"Who is there?" she shouted furiously.

"She's alive," the feminine voice.

"Yes, and you're on your own. I've got to go."

"What?" The single word was a shriek of amazement.

"Cath, I have to go, you've got to understand."

"Oh, right. Mine is the tough one this time so you're in a hurry."

"Cathy, it's the strangest thing, I can feel her. I'm being called, and I've assured her I'm on my way. On top of all that . . ."

"What?"

"I have to make a stop."

"Where?"

"At the nephew's house."

"The nephew?"

"We'll meet up shortly; I'll call you."

Rowenna heard the sound of a kiss. A quickish kiss; the kind a husband gave a wife before leaving for work in the morning.

"I'm insane. I don't need to kill myself; they'll just come and lock me up."

"You are insane," she heard. The female voice. Then there were hands, touching her.

She shrieked.

"I'm just trying to help you up!" she heard.

Why? What was going on?

She should have locked the door. She'd been warned over and over to do it. Who would have known that the people who broke into her house would be weird thieves who'd try to keep her alive rather than strangle or knife her?

"What are you doing here?" she demanded. "I'm going to call the police imme—"

"Why? To have them arrest you for trying to kill yourself? Suicide is against the law, you know."

"Who are you, and what is it to you?" Rowenna said. She'd seated herself on the desk chair. Now she was aware that the woman who plagued her had perched atop her desk.

"At least you *had* a child. And you're twenty-seven years old! You could have a dozen more."

Rowenna went dead silent for a moment. "A dozen more would never make up for one lost," she said quietly. "Ask any mother who has lost a child."

"No, one life can never make up for another. That's obvious. And I can't tell you that the pain isn't there, and that it isn't horrible. But do you know what I think?"

"Am I supposed to care?"

"If you're ready to kill yourself, you might as well listen to me first."

"I don't have much choice, apparently."

"No, frankly you don't. Unless you think you can will yourself to death."

"Who the hell are you?"

"You should know. You, of all people, should know."

"I—"

"I'm an angel on your shoulder, right now."

"What—"

"Cathy Angel. It's my name. Honestly. My husband, Don, just left."

Rowenna curled her fingers into her palms as her hands lay in her lap. "I don't care what your name is; you have no right to be in my house."

"You don't really want to die."

"I do."

"You don't."

"How do you know?"

"Because you know what you're planning is absolutely wrong. That you'll completely destroy, not just yourself, but the lives of those who love you."

"But my family is . . . gone."

"There are other people who love you. Those kids at the school will be haunted for the rest of their lives, wondering what they could have done, hurting. Rowenna, you don't want to die."

Rowenna gritted her teeth. "Fine!" she agreed. "You're right. I want to go back. I want to start my pregnancy over; I want to have a healthy child. I want to keep my parents and my baby off that airplane. I want—" She broke off. She could sense Cathy Angel— or whoever the hell the woman was—leaning toward her.

"Your marriage back?"

Rowenna inhaled sharply. "He left me!"

"Is that it? If you die, *he'll* be haunted, agonized, for the rest of his life?"

"No! No! That's the truth, he did leave me."

"Right. But maybe you didn't want to admit that you couldn't be perfect, even if you'd given birth to an imperfect child. Your husband knew you needed help. Admitting that meant abandoning your baby—to you. So you abandoned your husband instead."

"He's a grown-up! He—"

"Oh, Rowenna! Even grown-ups need help! Surely you've realized that now."

Rowenna was quiet for a moment, looking down at her hands, seeing nothing but shadowy gray. To her amazement, tears stung her eyes, then swept down her cheeks. The strange woman in her house made no attempt to tell her not to cry.

"You didn't cause your baby to be imperfect—though you've accused yourself of that over and over again because you remained so active until the birth."

"How could you possibly—"

"And you didn't cause that plane to crash. You know that!"

"But—"

"But your parents wouldn't have been on it if it weren't for you. You lived; they died."

"You can't understand the hurt."

"Indeed, I do."

"Then—"

"You need a good dose of Percodan, or Codeine. Tylenol III was always my favorite."

"*What?*"

"I'm speaking figuratively, of course."

"Ah. Then just what is it you think I should do for this kind of pain? What would work like a good dose of Codeine?"

"Call your husband."

"What?"

This time, Rowenna jumped out of her chair. She shook her head vigorously. "He left me. And I'm blind now!"

"Not worth staying with?"

"Now I'm—"

"You're a cripple, as your son was?"

"Yes, maybe, something like that."

"Not true. Forgive yourself, then forgive him. And when you've done that, you'll quit being afraid."

"I'm not afraid."

"Oh, are you lying! And on top of attempting to commit suicide! For a good Catholic girl, you are living dangerously."

"I grew up Catholic. That doesn't mean—"

"Oh, yes, you believe. You believe in the world, in the goodness out there—in beauty, in myth, in legend. Why else study angels?"

"You know, I really am incredibly aggravated. I want you out of my house—"

"Do you have an herbal tea in the kitchen?"

"What?"

"I really would love a good cup of herbal tea."

"If you know everything else—"

"I'll just check on the tea. You call your husband."

"I—I can't!" Rowenna said in a panic. "You're not listening—he left me!"

"Only after you left him."

"I never—"

"But you did. You left him to wallow in guilt and perfection and motherhood. You left him as distinctly as he left you. Then, when his pain was just as deep, you refused to share your agony with him. To learn to live with the pain together. Call him."

"If . . . if that were true," Rowenna protested, "he certainly wouldn't want to hear from me now! It's Christmas Eve; he probably has a date. He—"

"He's probably sitting home, remembering Christmas Eve last year, just as you were doing. I'm going for tea. Call him."

Rowenna wasn't sure how, but she was certain that the woman was gone, from her office at least. She moved her fingers across the desk.

Touched something metal. The gun. Her fingers wrapped around it. She set it in front of her, biting lightly into her lower lip. She would have hurt him; she knew that. She would have hurt Joshua badly if she had shot herself, killed herself. Had she wanted to hurt him even more than he had been hurt already?

Her fingers shook. She lifted the gun, set it down again. She reached across the desk.

The gun, the phone. Punishment, forgiveness.

If he would forgive her.

She had to forgive herself.

She was too, too afraid to dial . . .

She cleared her throat. "Excuse me! Whoever you are—Ms. Angel—when you're getting that tea, would you perhaps pour me a glass of wine?"

"Chicken!"

Rowenna managed a smile.

"Yes, very," she said softly to herself.

Still, she picked up the receiver and held it. She wasn't quite ready to dial.

But holding it was like . . .

Practice.

George Garrity sat in the upholstered leather chair in his living room, staring at the Christmas tree he had put up by himself. It was crooked; decidedly, it was completely half-assed. He'd put up some ornaments, some tinsel. He'd set an angel atop the tree.

He could have used help. He had kept believing that he just might get some.

But he hadn't.

Now he looked toward his son's room and waited. He didn't knock on the door—nor did he break it down, though doing that occurred to him from time to time. He remembered being a kid. He remembered peer pressure. He remembered the coming of the Beatles, the Rolling Stones, the entire British Invasion, the first Woodstock, Richard-Harris-in-MacArthur-Park, long hair, and all manner of creepy clothing. He'd always wanted to be a good dad, had had visions of being both tolerant and wise. He'd always wanted a son, had one, and now, to his great sadness and distress, he couldn't ignore what his son had become. A punk. He didn't know if Scottie did drugs regularly, but he was sure Scottie had tried a few. He was dragging the kid through high school, trying to keep him home and off the streets, while losing his cool at times and wishing to hell he could dunk his son in the nearest river.

When had it all gone so wrong? Some of it was easy to see. He and Jennie had divorced when Scottie was five. For a while, Scottie had been passed back and forth between them. Their differences had been irreconcilable, mainly because Jennie had grown bored with George. She didn't love him, and that was that. He hadn't hated her for not loving him; he couldn't get mad because she cheated or never wanted to be home. She just didn't love him. Nothing could change that. Still, once it had been accomplished, the divorce hadn't been bad. Scottie had split his time between his folks. But when he had turned ten, George had started dating Judith. Judith was, to George, a godsend. She never stayed with him when he had Scottie; it just wasn't right, she said. She tried in every way to be good for Scottie. Nothing worked. Because Jennie's romances began falling apart right and left, she started to tell Scottie that Judith was the one destroying the relationship between George and herself. Jennie undermined George's authority bit by bit, and Scottie, though a punk, was no fool. When Dad said no, he went to Mom. But he couldn't live with Mom because Mom had just latched on to a younger guy. She was traveling, or so she told Scottie. George was so tired and worn most of the time that he didn't totally blame Jennie, either. He had to be at fault, as well, for Scottie to be so damned hard to get along with. Judith tried to tell him that his son was sixteen now, and even if Scottie had been a bit brainwashed and spoiled by them both, it was time he started trying to be an adult. Not that the kid was a criminal as yet—or not that George knew about. Scottie was surly, and he was rude. He never ate dinner when George cooked; he waited until his father was in bed and raided the icebox for sandwiches and cookies. He was mean to Judith who quietly avoided him, and kept telling George to have patience with him. He'd had a few part-time jobs, a record shop, a fast-food joint, a movie theater. He'd lost all three for spending his working time hanging around with his black-jacketed, stringy-haired buddies. Not that George gave a damn about black jackets or hair. It was the sneers on the kids' faces when they grunted their hellos to him that bothered him. It was wondering where they went at night in their beat-up cars and what they kept in the trunks and glove compartments.

As George sat there, waiting, his son's bedroom door

cracked open. Scottie, a handsome enough kid, tall, lanky-lean, blue-eyed, with one of those under-shaved-upper-long punk hairdos, slipped out, closing the door to his room behind him. He started then, seeing his father sitting before the Christmas tree.

"Where are you going, Scottie?"

"Out."

"Out where?"

"Just out."

"Nowhere important?"

He shrugged. "With the guys."

"If it's nowhere important, maybe you could come with me for just a few minutes."

"Where?" Scottie asked, his blue eyes quickly shielded as he went on the defensive.

"To see your great-aunt."

Scottie stiffened, shaking his head. "In that old age home for penguins? No way."

"It's a home for retired religious. And I haven't asked you to go often. Aunt Mary is dying. They've just called me. They don't think she'll make it to Christmas Day. It would be a nice thing, Scottie, if you were to come with me. She—"

"She raised you, yeah, yeah, I know. Your folks died, she was off in the Peace Corps and came back and forgot about her religious calling until you were brought up. She's as sweet as mush, a great old lady, yeah, yeah."

"She's dying, Scottie."

"Well, we all die, don't we?"

George stood up, slipping into his jacket. "Yeah, Scottie, we all die. Some of us sooner than later."

"Aunt Mary is an old lady. A nun! She must be ready to die, meet her maker."

"Nobody is old enough to forget about love, Scottie," George said.

"Call your girlfriend, Dad. Judith will kiss your ass all over and make Aunt Mary feel like she's dying with friends."

"You watch your language, son."

"A fact is a fact, Dad."

"Scottie—"

"You gonna kick me out of the house? Your one and only son. You gonna throw me out so Judith can come live here?"

His father sighed, shook his head, and left.

In fact, Scottie was damned surprised his father hadn't already thrown him out so Judith could move in. It was coming, though. He should go live with his mom. He could, except that . . .

She was never there. His dad's fault. She was insecure. Trying to find younger men. She didn't like admitting she had a teenage son. She needed a husband. She couldn't hold down a job very well because she . . . she liked to party too much, Scottie admitted. Face it— she was a slut; his old man was a sour-faced dud.

The hell with Aunt Mary. He didn't need the scent of

old people and death. It was Christmas Eve. The guys were waiting. They had big plans for the night.

He started to reach for the door, then hesitated. He was feeling kind of low. He had a joint in his bedroom, under his T-shirts in the top drawer. He'd smoke it all by himself. Merry Christmas to me, Scottie thought.

He went into the bedroom and got out his joint. His dad was gone; he decided he'd have his joint in his dad's chair along with one of his dad's beers.

Seconds later he was curled in the upholstered chair in front of the Christmas tree. He popped the top of the beer, and reached for his pack of matches. Lit up the joint, inhaling deeply.

"Ho, ho, no! Merry Christmas!" he said. He wrinkled his nose, catching some of the smoke on its way out.

"Oh, yeah? Bah, humbug to you, young man!" snapped an angry voice. "Punk!"

And suddenly the beer can went flying.

Glistening liquid was pouring over his head in a gold and foam glow.

And his joint, doused, was hanging like a wizened Christmas ornament from his sodden lips. Scottie had been just about to inhale again.

He shrieked instead.

CHAPTER 9

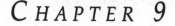

"Aunt Mary," George said gently.

He curled his fingers around hers, staring down at her. Her eyes had been closed; she opened them, acknowledged him. She still had the most beautiful eyes. She'd been the best parent in the world to him, always looking kindly at him with those eyes. What a pity he hadn't lived up to her hopes for him.

Her lips moved. He couldn't hear her speak. He bowed lower to try to hear what she was saying.

He heard the rattle of her chest.

Then her voice.

"Help me!"

"It's George, Aunt Mary. I'm here."

Her fingers curled around his. Tightly. So tightly that it hurt. And he realized.

She was afraid. So afraid of death. She had been his

strength so many times. She had given courage to so many. And now . . .

She was afraid.

He didn't know if he had the power to help her or not.

"What the fu—" Scottie Garrity began, leaping up.

"Don't say it, punk. Don't even think about saying it!"

There was nothing there; nothing at all but a voice. And Scottie, standing there and dripping, was suddenly slammed in the shoulder. "You snot-nosed little good-for-nothing! Everybody blaming everything on their parents these days, everybody dysfunctional. Well, kid, you've been loved as much as a man can love his child. You've—"

"Who the hell are you?" Scottie cried out, frightened. "Where the hell are you?" He stared at the sodden joint. "What the hell did they put in this shit?" he said, incredulous, his voice suddenly cracking.

"You just said it, kid," the voice told him a little more quietly, a little more gently.

Then, to Scottie's amazement, there was a man standing in front of him. Wearing a trenchcoat, as if it were cold outside instead of a perfect seventy-five degrees. He was a good-looking guy, not young, not old, maybe thirty-something.

Scottie gaped, froze, and fell back into his chair without even knowing that he moved. He tried to work his mouth.

"There's LSD in Dad's beer?" he said hopefully.

The man shook his head impatiently. "Listen to me, kid, and listen good, because you're not even on my list, and my time is limited. So you've had a few bad times. Your mom and your dad couldn't make it anymore. You're a big boy now, and what you do with yourself in the years to come is pretty much going to make or break your life. It would be great if I had some real time. Time to point out the way your dad took you to Little League, soccer; gave you guitar lessons, hung out, took the team for pizza and ice cream. All that little stuff. A couple of days wouldn't hurt, since it seems you've been nurturing that chip on your shoulder for years."

"I haven't got a chip on my—" Scottie began.

But suddenly, he did. It was brick, huge, dusty, moldy, sitting on his right shoulder.

He shrieked, leaping up. The brick chip crashed on the floor. The pieces lay there, then disappeared.

He looked at his visitor again.

"How'd you do that?"

The man shrugged. "Power of suggestion. I'm getting pretty good at it. But that's beside the point. I told you, I haven't got a lot of time. You're going to have to listen to me and believe what I say."

"But who—"

"It doesn't matter who I am; what matters is what I'm going to tell you. It's something not everybody gets a chance to hear. There is a heaven, Scottie, and certainly a hell, maybe several of each, I'm not quite sure of that yet. Heaven is on earth, just the same as hell. Hell can be the absence of love, and on that score, Scottie, you've cast yourself right into the pits. You aren't a real criminal—not yet—though stealing cash out of Salvation Army pots like you and the guys were planning on doing tonight could throw your ass in jail for some real time."

"How could you possible know—"

"Oh, come on, Scottie! You haven't figured out by now that I'm not from here?"

"But—"

"You've got one shot, Scottie. Listen to me tonight, and mend your ways. Got it?"

"But—" Scottie broke off with another shriek. The man in front of him appeared to erupt in flames, to lift his arms as if he were a fiery demon, reaching out for Scottie.

"No! Wait!" Scottie cried, falling to the floor, covering his head with his hands and his arms. "Please, I'm sorry, I'm so sorry, I'm not that bad, honest to God. I don't want to go to hell. Please, God, help me . . ."

There was no answer. He looked up at last. There was no one there. No one with him.

He breathed in quickly, exhaled. Felt like a fool. Looked around. Stared at the wet joint on the ground again, assuring himself that he must have gotten some bad stuff.

If only he could be sure . . .

But he couldn't. Shaking, he stood up. He needed a shower. And then . . .

He touched his face, stunned to discover that he was crying. He'd been scared. So scared. More scared than he'd ever been. He was going to take a shower. And then he was going to find his dad. Because, though he'd never realized it before, he'd never been scared when his dad had been with him. Never.

Despite her blindness, Rowenna had learned to use a phone with ease. Joshua, she thought, would have said it was because she was a typical woman, capable of chattering all day on the damned thing.

Now she discovered that she couldn't punch in the number. It wasn't because she didn't know the number. She did. When he'd left Florida, he'd gone up to live near his folks, just outside of Richmond. He'd gotten work at the university there. She'd had to dial him frequently enough for a while. Jeremy had still been alive; there had been the paperwork of the divorce. She knew the number.

On the third try, she pushed all the right buttons. The phone began to ring.

She was an idiot; what was she doing? There was no one in her house; she'd imagined the voices. She was losing it. Suicide was crazy, right? Yes, it was. And sometimes maybe a person reached a point where he or she did pull the trigger—or reach out for help. Unconsciously, she must have wanted help . . .

Two rings, three rings . . .

Now this was insanity. Suicide was less crazy. Joshua had surely gone on with his life by now. It was Christmas Eve. Why would he be home? He was a handsome man, intelligent, quick witted. Sincere. In a world where so much was lip service. Why hadn't she seen what was inside of him when she still had the power to see? She'd had to become blind and nearly dead to have any kind of vision at all.

Four rings, five rings . . .

Maybe he had a woman at his house. Maybe he was engaged. Maybe he'd remarried. Maybe he was in bed with someone even as she let the phone ring and ring . . .

Her hands were shaking. She started to hang up the receiver.

"No! No, let it go!"

Well, she hadn't imagined the voices in her house. The woman was back. She curled Rowenna's free hand around a glass. "Brandy. I warmed it and threw in a touch of cinnamon. It looked so good I went with it myself. Cheers!"

"He's not answering. This is stupid—"

"Let it ring a few more times."

"No, it's—"

"Hello?" It was a deep masculine voice at the other end of the wire.

Joshua. Rowenna tried to breathe, tried to talk. She

lifted her glass, slopping brandy. She managed to swallow some. It was good. Warming.

"Hello?"

Another sip.

"Hello? Hello?" Annoyance slipping into his voice.

"Talk!" Commanded her visitor. "I won't disturb you. I'll be back in the kitchen."

"Hello?"

He was going to hang up soon. Great. All she'd managed to do so far was make him angry.

"Is anybody there?"

"Jo-Joshua?"

Silence. "Rowenna?"

"I . . ." She twirled the phone cord in her fingers. "I—yes."

"Are you all right?" Anxiety laced his voice.

She could almost see his face. She longed to see it. "I'm fine, thank you."

She heard an audible sigh of relief, but then nothing more.

"Did I catch you at a bad time? I know it's Christmas Eve and all . . ."

"No."

"If you're entertaining someone—"

"Rowenna, it's not a bad time."

"Oh. Good."

Silence again. Where did she go from here?

"You're absolutely sure you're not busy?"

"Rowenna, I'm free."

She inhaled, exhaled. Tears suddenly streamed down her cheeks. "Joshua, I'm so sorry!"

"For what?"

"For everything. Oh, my God, for everything. For blaming you for Jeremy, for blaming me for Jeremy, for not being good enough for Jeremy, for being too good to him, for forgetting, for expecting too much, for not expecting enough. I'm just so sorry for everything I've done—"

"Rowenna, Rowenna, calm down, you're scaring me! Are you sure you're all right."

"Of course, I'm all right. No, I'm not. I'm blind, but I've learned to live with it. I'm all right, I'm not all right—"

"Rowenna, I'm coming down. I don't know how long it will take me to get a flight, but I'll be on the first plane I can beg, borrow, or steal my way onto, okay?"

"No, no, you don't have to—"

"You need help."

"I can't expect you, after what I've done to you—"

"Rowenna, I want to. You hurt me, yes. I didn't do so well by you either."

"Would you really come here now, for me?"

"Of course. Are you going to be all right until I get there?"

"I'll be fine." She'd been blind, she thought silently, and it had nothing to do with the fact that she couldn't see.

"I'm going to hang up to call the airlines. If I can't get

a plane soon enough, I'll get in my car and drive straight through, but I'll try to get a flight and be there by tonight. All right?''

She nodded, forgetting he couldn't see her.

"Rowenna?'' Anxiously.

"Joshua, you must have Christmas plans. A new life. I can't expect you to come here. I just had to tell you I was sorry. That I could finally forgive myself and you, and could hope you would forgive me.''

"Ro, you loved our baby. There's nothing to forgive in that.''

"Joshua . . . thank you so much.''

He was quiet for only a second.

"I love you, Rowenna. I have since I met you. I've never stopped loving you.''

Again, she couldn't speak. Couldn't find her voice. Her eyes stung furiously.

"Oh, God!'' she whispered. "I love you, too.''

"Hold tight. I'll be there as soon as I can.''

She hung up the receiver, sitting back. Her fingers touched the gun. She pulled them away quickly. She couldn't believe what she had been contemplating.

She started as the phone began to ring again. She stared at it, hesitating, afraid again. It was going to be Joshua. Telling her that it wouldn't work, that he couldn't come. He'd made a mistake.

Ring, ring, ring . . .

She jerked up the receiver.

"Rowenna, it's William.''

"William!" she said guiltily. She would have hurt him. So badly. What had she been thinking? It would have been such a cruel thing to have done.

"Rowenna, I know it's Christmas Eve. I don't know what you've planned, but this is important. Do you think you could help me out?"

"Of course. In any way I can. What do you need?"

"Do you think you could talk about angels to a friend of mine?"

Angels?

"I . . . of course," she murmured, still confused. Her cousin the priest wanted her to talk about angels? "Where are you, William?"

"At the home. I'll send a car for you. Oh, Merry-Almost-Christmas, Ro."

"You, too." He started to hang up.

"William?"

"Yes?"

"I love you, William. You're very special in my life."

"Thanks, Ro. You're very special to me."

He hung up.

She smiled, feeling for the cradle, replacing the receiver slowly and carefully. Oh, God, yes, *life* was special.

CHAPTER 10

D on had been with Mary since he'd left Scottie, not
at all sure what the kid would do, and not at all
sure his methods had been the right ones. Well, right or
wrong, he'd done his best. The kid had needed to be
shaken up a bit. Of course, he hadn't been assigned
Scottie, though someone should have been given the
kid. What a mess.

Now, as to Mary . . .

It hurt to be near her. To sit at her side, to feel the anguish sweeping through her. In his life, he'd never
known anyone so self-sacrificing; nor had he ever felt
such terrible fear. He tried to speak to her, to tell her that
it was going to be all right. He kept entering her mind,
but he couldn't tell if he had really touched her or not.
She was a powerful woman. She told herself she was
having morphine dreams.

He thought about appearing in material form to her,

GIFT RECEIPT

Barnes & Noble Booksellers #2275
131 Colonie Center
Albany, NY 12205
518-438-1728

STR:2275 REG:006 TRN:1504 CSHR:Joann G

BARNES & NOBLE MEMBER   EXP: 12/13/2017

Angel's Touch
 9781496708670   T1
 (1 @ RR.ZT)
                                    RR.ZT G

Connect with us on Social

Facebook- @BNColonieCenter
Instagram- @bncoloniecenter
Twitter- @BNColonieCenter

101.42A   12/06/2016 04:15PM

CUSTOMER COPY

and undamaged music CDs, DVDs, vinyl records, toys/games and audio books made within 14 days of purchase from a Barnes & Noble Booksellers store or Barnes & Noble.com with the below exceptions:

A store credit for the purchase price will be issued (i) for purchases made by check less than 7 days prior to the date of return, (ii) when a gift receipt is presented within 60 days of purchase, (iii) for textbooks, (iv) when the original tender is PayPal, or (v) for products purchased at Barnes & Noble College bookstores that are listed for sale in the Barnes & Noble Booksellers inventory management system.

Opened music CDs, DVDs, vinyl records, audio books may not be returned, and can be exchanged only for the same title and only if defective. NOOKs purchased from other retailers or sellers are returnable only to the retailer or seller from which they are purchased, pursuant to such retailer's or seller's return policy. Magazines, newspapers, eBooks, digital downloads, and used books are not returnable or exchangeable. Defective NOOKs may be exchanged at the store in accordance with the applicable warranty.

Returns or exchanges will not be permitted (i) after 14 days or without receipt or (ii) for product not carried by Barnes & Noble or Barnes & Noble.com.

Policy on receipt may appear in two sections.

Return Policy

With a sales receipt or Barnes & Noble.com packing slip, a full refund in the original form of payment will be issued from any Barnes & Noble Booksellers store for returns of undamaged NOOKs, new and unread books, and unopened and undamaged music CDs, DVDs, vinyl records, toys/games and audio books made within 14 days of purchase from a Barnes & Noble Booksellers store or Barnes & Noble.com with the below exceptions:

A store credit for the purchase price will be issued (i)

but George was there, and the priest, and he wasn't sure if that was what was he should do. He felt inane, wondering why he had been given Mary.

Angry that he had been given Mary.

What could he do for her, except hurt with her? She was dying. And he was an angel under rules that gave him only limited powers—the power of suggestion, the power to move objects, and the power to appear and disappear. He couldn't cure cancer. And since he couldn't, Mary was going to die.

Unless he gave her back life. At the risk of his soul. He paced the room.

George sat by Mary and held her hand. Don continued to feel at a loss. He thought of Rowenna then, with years of life ahead of her. Rowenna, who wanted to throw it all away . . .

Rowenna, who gave her great speeches about angels, making her students see the heavens and deities.

Rowenna! She couldn't see herself, but what fantastic visions she could create! Rowenna, who was related to the priest . . .

He smiled, and stared at Father William.

This was a piece of cake.

He implanted the thought in William to call Rowenna for help.

And William did, certain he had come up with the most brilliant plan ever.

George continued to sit at Mary's side.

Don clasped his hands behind his back. Pleased with

himself, relieved. He now had every confidence that
Rowenna was well and that Cathy would soon be here
with her. He knew his wife had fared better than he had.
Cathy was simply much better "angel" material than
he. He hesitated a minute, looking back at Mary.

What an incredible woman. She had such strength.
She had given so very much, done so much for others.

She deserved better than a struggling angel-candidate
such as himself. Dying, aged, there was something still
so beautiful about the woman. Her silver gray hair
streamed over her pillow. She inhaled and exhaled in
pain.

He turned back to the window, clenching his hands
into fists.

He'd forgotten one of the rules.

He could call on Gabriel.

Once!

This was only his second miracle. It should have been
so easy. It should have been incredibly simple. The easi-
est miracle in the world. Help a frightened old lady die.
Well, she was going to die one way or the other. And
there was nothing he could do about it.

He closed his eyes. *All right, Gabriel. This is it. Help me.
I'll calling on you now.*

Nothing happened. Mary let out something like a sob,
clinging to George's hand.

It's all right, Mary! he told her silently. There is a God,
he loves you.

Her fear came pulsing back at him like winter waves on a New England shore.

Afraid, afraid, afraid, oh, God, don't let me die, if there is a God, afraid, afraid . . .

A male nurse entered the room, checking the IV that sent a controlled amount of painkiller into Mary's veins. *I could twist the little knob,* Don thought. *Send the drug shooting into her veins . . .*

Kill her. End this agony quicker. Wouldn't that be helping her?

She's dying, what's the difference?

He suddenly realized that, though he was invisible, the male nurse was staring straight at him. He blinked, then realized that it was Gabriel, indicating that they should go out into the hallway to talk.

"You called on me?" Gabriel said. He sounded impatient.

"This is insane!" Don told him.

Gabriel arched a brow. "I would have considered this a fairly simple little miracle. Help Mary from this life into the next. Soothe away her fear."

"I should be doing something."

"There is no cure as yet for her cancer."

"Well, why didn't you just have me find the damned cure for her cancer?"

"We don't expect such intricate miracles from fledglings such as yourself."

"But—"

"It's simply not your job to discover the cure for cancer, all right?"

"That's what is so crazy! I don't understand what I'm doing here. This poor old woman is dying, and you're telling me there's nothing I can do about it!"

"I never said that."

Don was silent, staring at Gabriel.

"You mean I can take a chance and give life back to her, and lose—"

"You can."

"Can. But shouldn't, right?"

"Don, she's an old woman who has lived a long and fruitful life. Death is not an evil. It is a part of every man's life. In Mary's case, the time has come. Death seems cruel when it comes to a child . . . when it haunts a young woman such as Rowenna Trent. It tests one's faith when it comes for a young mother, a youth, a babe in arms. Death cannot come more gently than it does to those who leave this world by natural causes after having lived full lives."

"Then why does she hurt so badly?"

"She needs help. A guiding hand."

"I—"

"There are things you can do to allow death to come gently to her."

"But I feel . . . selfish. As if I should give up anything I could for her."

Gabriel threw up his hands in aggravation. "Look, I'm only supposed to spell things out for you to a certain point, but you have used your one chance to call on me for this, so I'll try to make you understand. It's Mary's time to die. Think about it. Do you believe she will suffer once mortal death has come? Look back at this gentle woman's life!"

"Yeah. Well, I hadn't thought I was such a louse myself!"

Gabriel arched a brow to him. "You want to compare yourself with this nun?"

"All right, all right."

Gabriel was still staring at him.

Don threw up his hands. "You can go now," he said, aggravated that Gabriel was still staring at him. "You're a busy angel, remember?"

He was startled to see that Gabriel actually smiled at him. "I am a busy angel. And you're not doing so badly yourself. Stopping by to see the kid was a nice touch."

"What?" Don looked at him, still steeped in worry about Mary, not sure of what Gabriel was talking about.

"Scottie Garrity."

"Oh. Oh, I . . ." Don shrugged. "Was that, ummm, fire stuff okay? I mean, I don't suppose an angel is really supposed to scare the sh—"

"Angels touch people in different ways," Gabriel said. "Actually, I rather liked it myself. Scottie needed a good swift kick in the behind. You did all right."

"Thanks."

"But now . . . Well, making Mary peaceful is your miracle. I've got to go. But you are, by the way, on the right track.''

"Thanks!"

Gabriel, in nurse's white, walked on down the hall-way, disappearing into mist.

Don stared after him, then reentered Mary's room.

He was startled to realize that Rowenna Trent had arrived while he'd been talking. She was seated at Mary's side, her fingers curled around those of the dying nun, and she was talking.

He didn't see Cathy, and for a moment his concern caused him to lose track of what was happening. He assured himself that his wife had to be all right—if "all right" could be the proper way to think of either of them; it was true that she was dead and they were both getting the gist of the angel thing. If he concentrated, he could surely find Cathy.

But he became aware of Rowenna speaking then, in her beautiful, soft, well-modulated voice.

"... they abound in the heavens by the hundreds, perhaps more. Angels, archangels, and more. They rise upon clouds of silky softness, billowing with a beauty untouched by even the greatest of our earthly artists. How could any palette re-create the splendor of the sky, the night, the stars? And remember, always, Mary, that God commanded the angels to be his voice to man. They touch us as we live, they have touched you, and through you, all those poor people helped by your hands. Mary,

I've heard this, read this, so very many times! When you pass over, they'll be waiting. Ready to take your hand, help you along. Pain will be gone; you'll walk on those clouds of satin and mist."

"My hand," Mary murmured. "An angel will take my hand."

Invisible, seated at her side, Don gently curled his own hand around Mary's.

To his surprise, she turned and looked at him. She smiled. She made no attempt to directly address him, to convince others that he was there. "An angel will take my hand," she said to Rowenna, her voice raspy.

A death rattle.

Yet even as Mary saw him, recognized him for what he was at last, they heard a slight commotion. Don saw Scottie Garrity—hair combed, tailored shirt tucked into clean blue jeans—come into the room. He was with an attractive woman in her mid-thirties. George Garrity was so surprised to see these two that he leapt up awkwardly from his vigil at his aunt's bedside.

"Scottie . . . Judith?"

The woman nodded, giving Scottie Garrity a squeeze around his shoulders. "Scottie came for me. George, you should have called me." Her voice was very low. She didn't want Mary to hear her. "I want to be with you in any way that I can—to help you."

George stared at his son, still amazed.

"Hi, Dad," Scottie said. He smiled a little remorsefully, a little ruefully, and walked over to Mary's bed, leaned down, and kissed her cheek. "Aunt Mary, it's me, Scottie. I love you."

"Scottie!" Mary whispered. "God bless you, child, God be with you . . ."

"And you too, Aunt Mary. You're already a saint, you know."

"Now, Scottie, only the Church—"

"You're a saint!" Scottie insisted, flirting with her somewhat. He grew more serious. "If you can come back as an angel, be with me, okay? I'll need you the most."

"Scottie!" George murmured.

"Now, George, leave the boy be." Mary gathered the strength that remained to her. She looked at Scottie and smiled. "What a lovely thought. We can't pretend that I'm going to get better here. I'm dying, and that's just as plain as day." She took a breath, and refused to let the pain stop her. "Scottie, I'd love to get to be an angel and come back and be with you! And I'm grateful to all of you for being here with me. So grateful. Scottie, stay there and hold my hand. Rowenna, you keep talking. George, stop crying and hold on to Judith. She loves you and it looks to me like she and Scottie have worked out a thing or two. George, you were a good boy, you're a good man, and I'm proud of you. Scottie, you're going to do just fine now, too." Her whispered voice faltered for a moment. "Rowenna, I haven't a lot of strength. You do the talking now. Then I need to rest. And have you all leave me with Father William."

She stared straight at Don again.

Smiled.

"Leave me with Father William. And the angels!" she said softly.

Mary weakened, weaved in and out of consciousness. They left her with Father William as she asked, but kept up their loving vigil.

At one point, as George and Scottie Garrity stood out in the hall, Scottie awkwardly approached his father. George even more awkwardly put his arms around his son and hugged him tightly. Scottie hugged him back.

Then Scottie started to cry.

George was already crying.

They didn't speak at first. Their awkward hugs said everything.

Scottie pulled away at last, drying his eyes with his sleeve.

"What did you get Judith for Christmas, Dad?" he asked.

George shrugged. "I'm not great with Christmas gifts. Perfume, a scarf. I'm not good with clothes—"

"How about jewelry?"

"What do you mean?"

"Don't you think you should buy her a diamond, Dad?"

George looked at his son, and shook his head. Scottie even looked different. He looked like a kid again. A boy.

His son.

He didn't say anything. He just put his arms back around his son. Hugged him again, certain that this time Scottie would protest. Eventually Scottie would, but for the moment he just hugged him back.

"I know how you love Aunt Mary, Dad. And I'm sorry for the way I've hurt you. I'm going to try to help you through this."

"You already have, son. You already have."

"Judith is really pretty cool, Dad. I didn't realize that she was so okay until I talked to her tonight. You should marry her."

"She has to agree to marry me. Maybe she will now, though. She wanted your blessing."

Scottie grinned. "My blessing. That's pretty cool, too."

George, glancing over his son's shoulder, saw that Father William had come quietly out into the hall. George cleared his throat. "William is motioning us back. Let's say goodbye to Aunt Mary. I pray there is a heaven—she'll be a saint."

"There is a heaven," Scottie said with certainty, following his father. He hesitated in the doorway to his great-aunt's room.

He was there. The man. The fire and brimstone man who had scared the—who had scared him half to death.

But now the man winked and smiled somewhat sheepishly.

"There is a heaven," Scottie repeated firmly to his father. "And Aunt Mary is going to have her place within it. Escorted there by an angel."

"Oh, Scottie, that's beautiful," Judith whispered softly to him. "Such a help to your dad right now!"

She smiled at him. He smiled back. It seemed so strange. His great-aunt was dying, and it was sad, but yet . . .

For the first time—in forever—it seemed that everything was going to be all right.

Cathy came in toward the end, slipping into the room to stand beside her husband, who had kept his place at Mary's side. Rowenna had stayed for hours; it was late now, and she had just been sent home.

Mary was at peace. Very near the end.

"Where have you been?" Don asked his wife.

"In Washington."

"Washington?"

She shrugged. "I had a few little errands."

He arched his brow.

She shrugged. "There was this guy with a little too much money for his own good, and he was about to fly off on Christmas Eve to meet some friends down here and party off to the Caribbean."

"Oh?"

"Well, he has a little girl. About seven years old. And she wanted him to stay home."

"Yes . . . ?"

"And I needed his seat on the airplane."

"Oh."

Mary opened her eyes suddenly, looking at the two of them.

"Angels?" she whispered.

"Don and Cathy," Cathy told her.

Mary smiled, moving her lips. "Help me," she whispered to the two of them.

"We're here," Cathy began. "We're both here, we're going to help you into the afterlife, the new life. We won't leave you until it's time . . ."

Mary shook her head, smiling. "Help me make them hear me, understand. I'm not afraid anymore. I can see you. God has given me vision at last. That poor beautiful dear creature who was here . . . I think I have one last gift to give. Please, get Father William, and my nephew. Help me make them understand."

That they could do.

They had become a great deal more practiced at the power of suggestion.

Between them, they brought Father William and George to Mary's side. Helped them hear the words she could barely whisper.

In the end, Mary didn't need help from either of the Angels. She had found her own peace. She held her nephew's hand, and that of Father William.

And in another ten minutes, she was gone. She slipped from them quietly and peacefully. Don and Mary both saw a trio of angels, decked in sweeping, Biblical splendor, hover over her. She smiled in death, then her soul arose.

She waved, maintaining that beautiful smile. Her eyes glowed.

There was no uncertainty within them.

No fear.

George Garrity cried softly, but his tears were good ones, natural ones. They flowed silently down his cheeks. He said goodbye to a woman he had loved. But he was going to be fine. His son and Judith were at his side.

"Shall we check on Rowenna?" Don asked Cathy.

"Oh, yes, we have to do that!" Cathy said. "And quickly," she added. She glanced upward, to the clock in Mary's room.

Christmas Eve was coming to a close. They had, perhaps, thirty minutes left.

And two more miracles to perform.

And if they failed . . . ?

They could not—would not! Don assured himself.

Could not . . .

"Rowenna?"

She heard his voice; Joshua's voice. Coming from the center of the living room.

"Josh?"

"Ro . . ."

His arms were suddenly around her. He swept her up. He held her tightly, so tightly. Whispered that he loved her, over and over again. She pressed his face between her hands. Felt him, touched him, again and again.

"How did you get here so quickly?"

"It must have been a miracle. I walked into the airport twenty minutes before a Delta jet left. There was a last-minute first-class cancellation, and I grabbed it."

"Oh, Josh . . ."

She tightened her arms around him.

"Ro . . ." His voice was constricted. "There's so much to say. I'm so, so sorry, too."

"No!" She pressed a finger against his lips. "My God, you can't be sorrier than me."

"I am."

"Can't be, I'm sorriest!" she said, and laughed. "But not tonight, it's Christmas Eve."

"I haven't a gift for you."

"You are a gift to me!"

He caught her arms, holding her a slight distance from him. "I forgot. I don't believe it, but I forgot—I was so excited to see you again. Rowenna, your cousin William just called. He said the nun who died had donor cards for just about everything in her body, but she insisted at the end that you were to get her retinas. She said you made her see, that she had been blind and you gave her sight, and she wanted you to see the world now through her eyes, wanted to return the gift."

"She can't . . . just do that, can she?" Rowenna asked.

"Apparently. I don't know. Your cousin, Father William, has connections, you know. If there is any possible way—if her eyes are still sound enough—you are to receive Sister Mary's gift of vision.''

Rowenna started to shake. He held her more closely. ''Rowenna?''

''It's Christmas Eve. I thought I had nothing left, and now I have life and sight and you. Oh, Joshua, I have nothing for you.''

''All I want for Christmas is to have my wife back. Marry me again, Rowenna?''

''Say yes!'' Hissed a pair of voices simultaneously.

''Did you hear something?'' Joshua asked, perplexed.

She shook her head, smiling. ''Just a pair of angels. Telling me to say yes. Yes, yes, yes, with all my heart. Oh, Joshua . . .''

She didn't need to see him to know his kiss. He swept her from the floor and into his arms.

She heard a soft sigh.

Then, she was dimly aware that her strange visitors left her.

She didn't need them anymore. She'd already been touched by them.

Touched by angels.

CHAPTER 11

"Angels we have heard on high,
Singing sweetly through the night,
And the mountains in reply,
Echoing their joyous cry . . .
Glo-ooooooo-ria,
In Excelsis, De-eee-o . . ."

Christmas music, once again, came sweeping through the night, emitted from a car radio. There were lights blinking on and off, intermittent sirens; there were people everywhere.

Don and Cathy had quietly departed Rowenna's only to find themselves back in the cold. A wind was rising; snowflakes were beginning to descend. It was a pretty snowfall, light, soft. The kind that would later be great for building snowmen, waging a snowball fight, sledding; and perhaps, in higher elevations, skiing.

"Where are we?" Cathy murmured.

Don looked around himself. They were in the middle of a disaster scene. It seemed that his heart took a sudden lunge, landing at the bottom of his stomach with a thud. They were back where they had begun. Nice touch. They had died here, but they'd been sent back to make miracles happen for others.

He slipped an arm around his wife. "We're back where we started. At the scene of the accident. Our car is just over there. Our bodies—unless they've picked them up—are on the other side of it."

"Oh," Cathy breathed out. She tried to speak emotionlessly. "You're right."

Don continued to stare toward their car. Cathy heard a moaning that seemed to be coming from close by. "Don?"

"Yeah?"

"Someone's hurt."

"Dozens of people are hurt. And some of them are dead," he reminded her bitterly.

"Near us. Don, please . . ."

He turned toward her, hearing the sound she was talking about. There was a crushed car near them, the driver's door hanging open on a twisted hinge. No airbag.

Cathy started moving toward the vehicle, stepping through high drifts of snow as quickly as she could. He followed her, realizing that most of the rescue workers were still crawling on top of the train's cars. A quick glance at this vehicle would lead most people to assume that any survivors had gotten out.

"Cathy, wait," Don warned. He could smell gas. Then he wondered what he was worried about.

He kept forgetting that they were already dead.

He hurried after her nevertheless, reaching the car with her, standing behind her and looking over her shoulder. The front seat was empty. The moaning was coming from the back.

Cathy slipped into the driver's seat, trying to look into the darkness behind it. Don started to struggle with the door handle.

"Who's in there, Cath?" he asked. "He or she is going to have to crawl over the front—"

"Don!"

"What?"

"It's a she, and she can't crawl over."

"Broken leg, arms . . . ?" Don ducked into the car along with his wife, staring into the back seat. There was a woman lying back there, panting, breathing, panting. She was bundled in coats. It took Don a few minutes to realize the problem.

"She's pregnant!"

Cathy laughed. "Very observant," she teased. "But not for long," she said worriedly. "Don, I think she's in labor." Cathy reached out a hand to the woman, who twisted and moaned. "Hey! We're here, we're going to help you, it's going to be okay."

"The baby is coming, the baby is coming!" the

woman gasped. She was small, blond, shaking and sweating. She was young, perhaps twenty-one.

"Your first?" Cathy asked her quickly.

"Cathy," Don warned, "this isn't the time for a friendly chat or an interview."

"I'm trying to keep her calm, Don."

"It's coming now!" the young blond cried. She gritted her teeth, tears rushed down her cheeks. She screamed suddenly, unable to bear the pain. "The baby is coming, we have to get out, it's coming, the gas, we're going to die, oh, God, oh, God, oh God . . ."

She lay back, screaming again. Cathy slipped over the seat in the very tight space. "Don, get the door open."

"All right."

He could see Cathy talking to the woman. Assuring her. Trying to help her. The space was so tight.

The smell of gas . . .

The blond woman was screaming again, gripping the seats, gripping Cathy. Cathy had her on her back, had her positioned properly for the baby to come.

Don stuck his head in.

"Cathy, the gas . . ."

"Don, the head is out!"

"Do something."

"I'm doing it, I've just never had obstetrics, I'm trying not to kill her."

Cathy's words were drowned out by another scream.

"The shoulders are here!" Cathy cried. "One more push, come on, come on . . ."

"I can't, I can't, I can't, I—"

"You have to! Dammit, now!"

The woman must have pushed.

But there was no little baby cry.

"Cathy, now, or she's dead!" Don said.

"Get the door," Cathy agreed.

Don jerked on it. Stubbornly, it remained fast. He started to struggle with it again before remembering that he was an angel. He set his hand upon it, stared at it, willed it to open. It popped free like greased lightning. He reached in for the woman, dragging her out by her feet. He hefted her into his arms and started to run, Cathy, with the infant, at his side.

They covered ten feet quickly, twenty . . . a hundred yards.

Then the car exploded. Fire shot up into the night. Pieces and splinters of the twisted, burning metal began to rain down around them. Others started screaming; rescue workers began shouting.

Don had fallen into the snow with the woman, thrown down by the force of the blast. He straightened himself, dragging his weight from her. She was so pretty, so young, and so terrified. She looked up at him, amazed at first to be alive. Then her eyes filled with waves of tears.

"My baby . . ."

"Lady, you're alive!" Don whispered to her softly.

"And the baby is . . . a little girl!" Cathy said, coming

up around Don. He stared at his wife, frowning. He'd been convinced that the child had been born dead.

But now he heard the infant gurgling. Cathy had managed to wrap it in her scarf. It was—in Don's eyes—a sodden mess. It had hair, but what color it was he couldn't begin to tell.

The blond mother shrieked out, hysterical with happiness, reaching for her infant. She wrapped her child in her arms, shaking, crying.

"Oh, thank you, oh, God, thank you, oh . . ."

"Cathy, we've got to get her help. That baby could freeze to death, this lady could still be bleeding."

"We'll get—" Cathy began, but then they heard the man shouting.

"Evelyn! Evelyn!"

He was young, as blond as his wife, with soft blue eyes, terrified. He was standing in the snow, a firemen with the "jaws of death" standing beside him. He was staring at the burning car, stricken. He fell down to his knees in the snow, his cry of anguish bursting through the relentless Christmas carols that continued to spill cheerfully from a car radio.

"My husband . . . Robert! Robert, here!" the woman called out, "Oh, Robert."

Don caught Cathy's hand. Simultaneously, they exerted their power to disappear, and did so quickly. They walked swiftly and silently away as they watched the young man run to his wife, fall to his knees again at her side, sobbing. The firemen were quickly with them, ready to rush mom and child to the hospital.

"They're going to make it, Don," Cathy said.

"Yes, they are."

"Oh, sweetheart, don't be bitter!" Cathy said softly.

Don stood straight, looking back on the young couple and their newborn child. "I'm not, I'm happy for them."

"Being angels isn't so bad."

"I know. It's just that I felt . . ."

"What?"

"I don't know. That we had more living to do. That there was more we might have done, somehow."

"We've done very well tonight."

He paused in the snow, drawing her against him, kissing her forehead and the tip of her nose. "I know, we've done well. It's just that—"

"What?"

"Oh, my Lord. What time is it? We're running out of time! We helped that woman, but was that what we were supposed to do? Cathy, we've got about fifteen minutes left. I don't mind being an angel, as long as I'm an angel with you. I made that level of heaven by your shirttails, remember?"

"Don, I'm convinced you really made it on your own."

"Let's not take chances. What does the list say?" he asked.

Cathy reached into her coat pocket, staring at their list.

"Well, what does it say?"

"Don, rescue Cassandra, Cathy, help the boys."

"Rescue Cassandra, help the boys," Don muttered with disgust.

"Maybe the blond woman—"

"Her name was Evelyn, remember?" Don said. He threw up a hand in disgust. "Now I know why there's so much ridiculous red tape and confusion in the world. They always say that policy drifts down from the top! Who is Cassandra? What boys?"

"I don't know about Cassandra, but I think I know who the boys are. The children, Don. Don't you remember? They were in the train car, six of them. The kids from St. Mary's."

"We already helped them. They're out of the train, remember, we brought them out and set them down in the snow . . ." Don broke off, staring toward a mangled railroad car. They had taken the kids out and set them on the nearby embankment, but the railroad coach had twisted to the opposite side of the tracks from the one on which they had been smashed into the train. Either from loosening in the impact or the weight of the fallen snow, the embankment had sunk. Two of the derailed cars from the train had fallen like a bridge over the gaping hole that had been created.

"How the hell . . . ?" Don began.

For once, Cathy made no comment on his language. "Maybe the area had been dug out once for the subway system," Cathy murmured. "But they must be down there."

Don caught her hand, and they raced across the newly fallen snow.

There were rescue workers on the job, a multitude of them, but since the car had exploded, they were focusing their attention nearer the blaze that threatened to spread through the night. Their efforts were hindered by the snow, the sheer magnitude of the accident, and the confusion that came out of having a number of different agencies trying to help. One of the train's coaches was on fire; something besides Evelyn's old automobile had exploded. Don assumed that a gas tank had ruptured somewhere in the mess the train had become, causing the second fire. The train had been nearly full, at holiday capacity. And at least fifty automobiles had become involved in the accident—half on the one side of the tracks, where they had piled into one another and the train, half on the other, where the derailed railroad cars had jackknifed into the automobiles. Complicating the mess was the weather, the darkness—and the noise.

Now "Rudolph the Red-Nosed Reindeer" was coming over the car radio that refused to die. Sirens kept shrieking in the night. Rescue workers called out to one another.

So much noise . . .

Victims, crying, shouting . . .

Sobbing.

Don scrambled over one of the fallen railroad

coaches, reaching down to help Cathy up and over the twisted pile of metal and wreckage. He then leapt down to the soft, snow-covered earth on the other side. They were off the road, away from the smashed cars. Here the earth had sunk under the weight of wreckage or nature. More snow had fallen upon the broken earth, and with flakes falling still, it was almost impossible to see beneath the bridgelike twist of railroad cars that stretched over the fallen earth.

Cathy pulled back on Don's hand. "Don't go near those rail coaches!" she warned.

"Cathy, we have to crawl below them."

"They could fall."

He paused, seeing her point. The railroad cars barely spanned the chasm. The least amount of weight set against these tons of metal could send them crashing down.

Crushing any life form whatsoever beneath them.

"Come over here, Cath, we can use the snow, slide down it."

She caught his hand, following him. They found the little tract of snow, sat in it together, and braced as they started to whip faster and faster downward beneath the train's cars. They catapulted into darkness. Don's feet thudded against something that spoke.

"Ohhh . . . Ouch!"

"Hello, boys? Can you hear me?" Don asked.

"Hey, it's help!" someone said.

He thought he had a lighter in his pocket. There was

no smell of gas or kerosene here. He flicked it on. Caught and entangled in metal, luggage, strewn clothing, tires, wires—and more—was a little boy of about six. Don lifted the lighter. There were more of them. The group they had met before and had left above on the ground.

"Can you help us?" the boy demanded. He was about ten, Don thought. "We've been afraid to move." He was young, but bright. He pointed upward. "If too much snow shifts, that will fall."

"There are six of you?" Don asked.

"Me and my brothers."

"You're all brothers?" Cathy said.

The boy nodded. "Yeah, out of St. Mary's."

Cathy was next to him in the snow. She placed her hands on his face, studying his eyes. "I can't believe no one has adopted you!" she murmured.

"Cathy, we're in the middle of a disaster here," Don reminded her.

"I know, but—"

"We're not splitting up," the boy said stubbornly. "We won't, and we've all sworn to make it hell for anybody who tries to get us to do that, understand? Besides, most of the time, I can take care of these guys myself. As soon as I'm eighteen, I'm getting the best job I can, and I'm adopting my own family. We won't be split up. Mom didn't want us split up, understand?"

"I sure as hell have no intention of splitting you up,"

Don said wryly. "I'm going to try to save your lives; then you can grow up and adopt them, okay?"

"Don—" Cathy said.

"He's cool, lady. He's cool," the boy said, grinning. "I'm Brenden, those are my brothers Sean, Michael, Harry, David, and Pete. Oh . . . I forgot the girl!" he said, stricken.

"The girl?" Cathy asked, looking around. She saw a little girl, as dark haired as the boys were light, curled into something like a fetal position not far from where the others hunched in the wreckage and snow. She was perhaps nine, with huge light blue eyes. Her coat was ripped; she wore one glove. She didn't seem to notice.

"Tell me," Don said, "Please . . . might this young lady be named . . . Cassandra?"

"Yeah, that's her name," Brenden said, glancing at Don curiously.

"Yes!" Don said, clenching his fingers into fists and then drawing two down in a victory sign. "Yes!" he repeated. "Cathy, we can make this!" He flicked his lighter and glanced at his watch again. "Pete's the little guy. Slither here, Petey, David—"

"David has a broken leg," Brenden said matter-of-factly.

"You get Pete, I'll get David," Cathy said, her look warning him that she was simply the more gentle person.

Or angel.

He nodded to her, lifting up little Pete. He was an

angel, but getting back up the slide of snow that was quickly chilling into ice still seemed a monumental task. And Cathy, behind him, was huffing and puffing quite a bit for a supernatural being.

As they reached level ground once again, Cathy saw the nun, who had passed out earlier, sitting up now, very lost, sobbing.

"Over there," she told Don.

They ran. The nun looked up. "Oh, God, thank you! The rest of them . . ."

"We're going back. Look, they've fallen into that depression," Don said.

"Beneath the cars?" the sister demanded anxiously. She, too, instantly saw the danger.

"Try to get some more help, will you?" Don said. He caught Cathy's hand again. They ran back. Brenden already had little Cassandra drawn from her position. He was trying to shove her upward by her well-padded butt, his little brothers at his side, trying to help.

"Got her!" Don cried.

"Someone else, come with me, now!" Cathy commanded.

"Sean, get your butt in gear!" Brenden told one of the littlest of the crew. Sean obediently went to Cathy.

They made a second, slow, tedious ascent up the ice.

"There's help coming," the sister told them. She had David stretched out by her side. "They're getting ropes so they can get down there," she said anxiously. She stared at Don and Cathy.

David tried to rise, to look at the two of them. "The snow is so slick. It's icing," he said.

"It's okay, David," Don assured the boy.

"It will be," Cathy promised, winking at David, who almost managed a smile in return.

Time was of the essence. For all of them.

"Great. We'll take another run while we're waiting," Don said. He caught Cathy's hand. They hurried back again.

"They're such beautiful children, Don, all of them. So brave. They've been hurt so badly, and they still cling to one another. And they were trying to take care of poor little Cassandra as well."

"We have to hurry, Cathy."

She suddenly stopped, tugging at his fingers.

"Don, it's starting to slip."

Even as she spoke, they heard a grating sound. Cathy cried out; the train cars slid . . . caught in the earth. Stopped again.

"We could call on Gabriel," Cathy whispered.

"I . . . er . . . can't. I already have."

"I can."

"Cathy, we're all right. I'm going down now." He released her fingers and, this time, lay flat in the snow, trying to move as quickly as humanly—or inhumanly—possible. Once again, Brenden had the last two, Harry and Sean, ready to go. "Give me Harry," Don said.

Cathy nearly catapulted into him. "Sean, grab Cathy

there. Brenden, you've got to try to scratch your way up behind us, okay?''

"Yep, I gotcha," Brenden said.

Brenden knew. The cars were about to come crashing down on him.

They started back up again.

Heard a groaning of metal. A rasping, ripping of rock, of concrete perhaps.

The cars were slipping again.

"Don!" Cathy cried. "We have the power to move objects."

"It's one big, damned object, Cathy!"

"We've got to try—together."

They were nearly at the top. Don shoved a boy up, reached for Cathy's charge, shoved him as well. He tried to reach for Brenden and concentrate on moving the railroad cars.

The car began to shift, to fall, to rise . . .

A sudden, hideous shriek of metal ripped into the night as the railroad cars gave. Don screamed himself, reaching for Brenden.

The rail cars ripped out earth and trees and concrete as they plummeted down.

He didn't quite have Brenden.

The little boy slipped down the ice. He wasn't buried beneath the train cars though. He went hurtling down to land atop one with a heavy, deadly thud.

CHAPTER 12

"Get him up, get him up!" Cathy cried hysterically.

But by then, the rescue crews had come. They didn't seem to see her or Don, they clattered past them with ropes and pulleys and the like.

Don caught hold of Cathy, drawing her a distance from the scene where the men quickly arranged a line and lever. One of the rescue workers was attached to it and lowered slowly—very slowly—downward.

He reached the boy. A canvas stretcher was lowered down to the rescue worker so that he could bring the boy up. By that time, Brenden's brothers had come one by one to the scene. They watched in silence.

Tears streamed down little Sean's cheeks.

"Oh, please, please, please, please, God," Sean started to whisper.

The men drew the stretcher bearing Brenden back up to the level surface. Brenden's coat was loosened.

"He's dead," Someone said. "Poor kid."

"No!" Harry shrieked.

"No, no, no," the others chimed in.

"Hey, kids, we'll try, honest to God, we'll try," the rescue worker, a kindly looking man of about fifty said. "Damn it, someone get a real doctor over here now!" he roared. He knelt down in the snow. Closed Brenden's little nose with his fingers, pursed his mouth, and started to try to breathe for Brenden.

"He's dead," Cathy said dully.

"Cathy, we did what we could."

"Don." She spun on him, and he saw what lay in her eyes.

"Cathy, no. Gabriel said we had the power, but that we couldn't use it. Cathy, no . . ."

"Oh, God, Don, I love you so much! But that little boy was such a fighter! His brothers, what will happen to them all now? I do love you, but please understand. I have to do this. Don, please . . ."

"Cathy, oh, God, no!"

"Don!"

"What about us?"

"Forgive me, I do love you."

"Hell is the absence of love!" he whispered.

"I will always love you!" she said.

He sank down to his knees in the snow, broken himself. She fell down in front of him. "Oh, Don, he's a little boy. With so very much to live for. They'll be split up without him. He was so good, so brave. They're all so beautiful, but he's special."

"Cathy, I love you."

"Don . . ."

He heard the anguish in her voice. Knew what it cost her to leave him.

Knew that she felt she had to. Cathy. She had always loved kids so damned much. Had always had their trust.

They had been coming to this. All night long.

"Cathy . . ." he whispered. He could see their car. By its side, covered in snow, would be their bodies. So many miracles.

None tonight for them.

Unless . . .

Oh, God, yes.

There could be a miracle.

He kept staring at the car. At their dead bodies.

Cathy slipped her arms around him. "Don, forgive me. I have to do this. Please . . . hold me!" she whispered. He did so.

He couldn't let her go.

He had to let her go.

He knew what to do.

She eased his arms from her and stood. He could hear her silently willing Gabriel to appear.

This time, he appeared in what Don had always imagined would actually be "angelic glory." His robes were mauve and white and gold, the silver of his wings seemed heightened by the glow of the fires all around them. He appeared in a gust of mist, and stood before them, waiting.

"Ah, Cathy. Don. You don't need me now, you've accomplished your miracles. It's very nearly midnight."

"I need your help desperately," Cathy said.

"For?"

"That little boy." She pointed toward Brenden and the man working so diligently to save him.

Gabriel looked from the boy to her.

"He's dead."

"Yes, but the miracle was to help the boys—"

"And you did. It's a miracle any of them are going to live."

Cathy shook her head strenuously.

"I was told to help the boys," she told Gabriel evenly. "That little guy is nowhere near grown up himself, and he gave everything he had to save his brothers."

"So you want to give him life."

"Yes."

"I'm warning you—"

"I have to do this!" Cathy whispered vehemently. She looked at Don.

She needed his help. Needed his strength, he knew. He stood behind her, setting his hands upon her shoulders. He felt so cold.

So frightened.

"I'm still warning you," Gabriel said, "that you put yourself into grave peril—"

"I understand, I've heard your warning. But I'm not asking you for advice. I'm asking you what I must do to give him life."

"I gave you a booklet to read, you know," Gabriel told her.

"I'm sorry. I haven't really had the time to go through it properly," Cathy said, exasperated.

"You're going to let her do this?" Gabriel asked Don.

Strangely calm, he said, "I've argued with her. But I haven't really the power to stop her, do I?"

Gabriel stared at him for a long moment, then sighed. "Go to the child. Hold his hand. Will life into him."

"That's it?" Cathy asked.

"You've learned to project thoughts and images into the minds of others. To move objects. This is just the same. Concentrate, and will life back into the boy."

"All right," Cathy said. She turned to Don. Tears sprang into her eyes again. "Please understand. I have to do this."

Don watched her gravely, nodding. "I know, Cathy. I know. That's one reason I love you so deeply. So very much." He enveloped her in his arms. Crushed her against him. Whispered, "I love you, Cathy. For all eternity. Somehow I will find you—come heaven or hell."

"You haven't much time," Gabriel commented.

Don turned to him. "Do you mind?"

Once again, Don turned to his wife. Placing his back

between themselves and Gabriel, he kissed Cathy, slowly, tenderly. She returned his embrace, his kiss. Then she suddenly tore from him. And ran across the snow to the place where the rescue workers still worked over the young orphan, Brenden. She slipped through his brothers, pressed aside by the paramedic who thumped on the child's heart, tried to get oxygen back into his lungs.

The children were jostled, but they didn't seem to notice. And Cathy, invisible, was there.

An angel in the snow. She had never been more beautiful. She took the young boy's hand in hers.

Looked back to her husband one last time.

"I love you," she mouthed.

"I love you, too," he mouthed back. For eternity, Cathy. You'll never know just how much.

Then he turned to run himself.

In a different direction.

He had the power to give life back. Once. Only once. He could give life back to a stone-cold corpse.

And he intended to do so.

Gabriel caught his arm. "What do you think you're doing?"

"Giving life back."

"To Cathy?"

"Of course. Will it work? It will work, right? But I should hurry before whatever could happen to her happens?"

Gabriel released him. "Remember you risk your soul."

"I have no soul without her. But answer me, please. Will it work?"

To his amazement, the angel smiled. "Yes, it will. I rather thought this was what you intended."

"You're not going to try to stop me?"

Gabriel shook his head. Don smiled wryly. "You never really did like me a hell—sorry, heck—of a lot."

"On the contrary, you've come a long way."

"Thanks. And thanks for you help." Awkwardly, he extended a hand to the angel. Gabriel accepted it. Shook it. "Hurry," Gabriel told him.

Don nodded, and started running through the snow himself. He reached their car, imbedded now in the snow. He crawled, slid, and slithered over it, falling into the snow where his and Cathy's bodies lay.

He ignored his own, brushing the snow fervently from Cathy. God, how lovely she was, even in death. He drew her from the snow into his arms, dusted her cheeks. Kissed her cold lips. "Ah, Cath, you told me you were cold. I can warm you, my love." He closed his hand around hers and looked toward the night sky, the stars appearing there despite the snowfall.

"Thank you, God, for this chance to save her!" he whispered.

He closed his eyes for a moment, admittedly afraid of what his future in death could be . . .

"Live, Cathy, live!" he whispered. He kissed her lips again, breathing his power and warmth against them.

"Live . . ."

And in his arms, she suddenly choked.

And began to breathe . . .

CHAPTER 13

Cathy Angel very slowly opened her eyes. She was cold; she was sore. She blinked, and realized that there were all manner of people staring down at her. It was night; there was shouting. She could see flames leaping into the air, feel snow upon her face, feel heat, pain, relief . . .

She tried to move.

"Hold still, lady. They say you went into that pit a dozen times. The kids are okay, there's a mountain of rescue workers here, you just take it easy now, eh?"

She couldn't do that; she tried to rise. She shook her head. She felt as if a mist of confusion was drifting through her mind.

Christmas Eve, Fifth Avenue. She'd been trying to hurry to meet Don because she knew the holiday traffic would be getting to him, night would be falling . . .

The accident. The truck had crashed into them; they'd plowed into it.

She'd . . .

She'd died, hadn't she . . . ?

She could vaguely remember the children. Yes, she must have thought she was dead. But they'd lifted the children from the train . . .

Or dragged them from a pit?

The boys. She remembered the boys clearly. Brenden, Harry, Sean, Michael, David, and Pete. Brave Brenden, so little to be using such tough talk, yet so determined and strong. Until . . .

He had fallen.

"Brenden . . ." she murmured.

"The boy is going to be okay. Thanks to you and your husband."

"My husband!" Cathy whispered. Her eyes widened. She looked around desperately. "Don . . . where's my husband?" she asked.

The workers around her stared uncomfortably at each other. Cathy looked across the snow.

Don.

He lay on his back. His face was nearly as white as the snow. It seemed that he slept. At peace. "Don!" Cathy whispered.

"Wait!" someone called, trying to stop her.

They could not. She crawled desperately through the snowbanks to his side. "Don? Don?"

She touched his face. His handsome features. He was cold. Colder than the snow, like ice, like . . .

Death.

"Don!" She shrieked his name. Heedless of the snow, of the world around her, she drew him into her arms, pressing her lips to his, touching his forehead. "Don! Damn you, don't leave me, *don't leave* . . ."

She started to sob. Great tremors wracked her; hot liquid tears began to flow down her face.

Splashing on his forehead, his cheeks.

Gabriel brought himself into human form to watch the accident scene unfold.

He'd been at this many, many years. He was no stranger to pain, to death. And yet . . .

He wished that he had the power. To give life.

But he did not.

He was the messenger angel. Trusted, beloved. But he didn't have the power to give back life.

"Dear God . . ." he prayed. There was no actual form to his prayer, yet he suddenly felt light and warmth, and knew that he was not alone.

"He loved her."

"He was a good man."

"Yes, better than I realized. I wish I had the power to . . . help."

"But you don't."

"Perhaps he needn't perish forever," Gabriel suggested.

He heard laughter. A soft chuckle that still filled the heavens with thunder.

"He was a good man, indeed. With a few lessons to learn."

"And those learned too late," Gabriel said sadly.

"Maybe not."

"He had but one chance to give life. He gave it as he felt he had to, just as she gave it as she felt she had to."

"Yes."

"But now . . . Oh, it is heartwrenching, isn't it, my Lord?"

"Maybe not so sad."

"But they've both used their power—"

"Ah, but in the end, my dear servant, *I* am the ultimate power."

"Yes, my Lord. Of course."

And Gabriel smiled. "I don't mean to be presumptuous, sir, but the way everything has gone tonight with Cathy and Don Angel—could it be that this is what you had planned all along?"

"It is what I hoped all along. You must remember, I have given mankind—and the angels, if you'll recall—free will. And free will does leave things in the open a bit now and then."

"Yes, sir."

"Carry on, Gabriel, if you will."

"Immediately, sir."

Gabriel hurried over to Cathy and Don.

———

"May I see what I can do?"

Cathy looked up, startled. The man appeared to be a doctor or a paramedic. He was dressed in white, even to the huge fur-lined overcoat he wore. As stricken and terrified as she was, she noted his appearance, for he was a striking man. Beautiful might have been a more apt description, he was so very handsome. He seemed to radiate light, and warmth.

And she trusted him, instantly.

She moved back, still studying his face.

"Please!" she whispered brokenly. "Please . . . make him live."

The man nodded. He bent over Don, going about the normal procedure for resuscitation. He felt her watching. He paused, smiling at her, reassuring her.

"The breath of life," he murmured.

Don was still so white . . .

"Help him, please!" Cathy whispered.

The man stood, looking down at Cathy. He smiled.

"You still have the power."

"I don't."

"Hold him, warm him. Love him. Will him to live."

Cathy looked back to Don, tears in her eyes. When she looked up, the man was gone.

She drew her husband back into her arms . . .

She nearly jumped when he groaned. "Cathy?"

"Don!"

He looked up at her. Smiled slowly. She started to cry

again, raining kisses all over his face. He slipped his arms around her, holding her in return.

"Oh!" she cried suddenly. "Are you broken anywhere? I mean, did you break anything. Are you—"

"I seem to be fine. I've had the weirdest dreams, though."

"They weren't dreams."

"What?"

"We must have been all right immediately after the accident. Don't you remember? We pulled the children out of that pit that formed after the crash. Maybe we inhaled too much smoke or something . . . Oh, Don! The children."

She'd been holding him. Holding him as if he were the most precious thing in all creation. Assuring herself that he was well, fine, whole, all in one piece . . .

Then suddenly, she was up.

Nearly clunking his head right down upon the ground.

"Don—"

He stood beside her, rubbing his head. Dear Lord, but he'd had the strangest damned dreams. He'd died, he'd gone to heaven. Not quite heaven.

"Don, come on. We've got to see about the children!"

Cathy started hurrying on as he paused for a second, shaking his head.

He stared at their car. Shook his head again.

It was a miracle they were alive.

Miracle . . .

He looked across the wreckage, he saw a doctor in a white coat bent over a man. The doctor glanced his way. A handsome man. With a face so arresting it was startling. Like light. Brilliant . . .

The man smiled suddenly, gave him a thumbs-up sign.

And Don knew. It hadn't been a dream.

He started hurrying over toward the angel, Gabriel. By the time he reached the place where Gabriel had been, the man was sitting, holding his head. The angel was gone. Don hurried after him. Tapped him on the shoulder.

When he turned, Don saw a stranger, someone he had never seen before.

"Sorry!" He said softly.

"Hey, we're all pretty confused here," the man said.

Don nodded. The man hurried on. Then Don felt a tap on his shoulder. He turned.

The doctor-angel was behind him. Don inhaled. Tears stung his eyes. He felt weak, as if his knees were going to give.

"Thank you," he managed to whisper.

The angel smiled. "Don't thank me. You know that supervisor you wanted to see earlier?"

Don smiled, nodding.

"You might want to thank him." Gabriel nodded at Cathy. "Go get your wife, huh?"

"Yes. I'm going to get my wife. And my boys."

"*Your* boys?"

"Yeah. The kids. Great kids, aren't they? It's strange, I always thought I'd be an okay father if I could start with a baby. I mean, we were always trying for a baby. But I've . . . I've touched these little guys. The oldest one is great. Oh, I just realized, I guess we should take the little girl, too, huh?"

"Sons—and a daughter. Sounds good to me," Gabriel said. "A pack to want the car on Saturday nights. A little girl to cook cupcakes for Dad, then break his heart when she finds the love of her life."

"Cathy would be great with a little girl."

"Cathy would be great with any kid. And so would you."

"Yeah?" Don said to Gabriel.

"Yeah. But are you sure? Seven kids?"

Don shrugged. "You only go around once, right?" he said.

Gabriel nodded. "Unless there's a miracle."

Don grinned. "Thanks again!" he whispered. He turned, knowing that if he looked back, the angel would be gone.

And he wouldn't see him again. Not in this life.

There, up ahead, was Cathy. She was on her knees in the snow with the penguin-like nun, the little girl Cassandra, and all the boys. They were talking excitedly. It looked as if they had known one another a long, long time.

Don paused. He looked upward. Heavenward.

He closed his eyes.

Thank you. Oh, God, thank you.

Christmas. The gift had been life. And more.

Faith.

He glanced at his watch. Twelve-O-One.

He started running again. Plowed into his wife where she knelt in the snow. She landed flat back against it.

An angel in the snow, he thought.

He pounced down upon her, wondering what he was doing to them if they had a lot of cuts or bruises. But at the moment, it didn't matter.

"Merry Christmas, Cath!" he told her, and kissed her.

She hugged him, kissing him in return, while the kids all cheered.

"She's pretty cool, huh?" he asked them all, pausing specifically to look at Brenden.

"Sure," Brenden agreed.

"She'd make a great mom, huh?"

Brenden stiffened. "We won't split up—"

"What did you say, Don?"

"I said you'd make a great mom."

"Don!" Cathy breathed. "These are big guys!"

"All potty-trained."

She gasped. "You mean it?"

Don turned on Brenden, wagging a finger sternly. "You get a sister, too. We can't leave Cassandra out of this. And you all be decent to her, you hear?"

"All of us?" David said incredulously.

"We—we can deal with a sister," Brenden said.

"All of us?" David said once again.

"All of you!" Cathy shrieked. Rising from the snow, she pounced on Don in return, kissing his forehead, his cheeks, his lips.

The kids cheered.

"Cathy, Cathy, let me up!" he pleaded.

She sat back. "Don, seven children?"

"Well, if you can't handle it—"

"I can handle it, I can handle it!" she cried, staring at him. She shrieked again.

Pounced on him again.

Kissed him again.

Oh, God, he loved his wife.

He managed to bring them both back up, covered with the snow.

He looked at the group of kids, then to the sister who had been in charge of them.

"They are up for adoption, right?"

"Oh, yes!" She exclaimed, clapping her hands together gleefully. "Oh, yes! This is so wonderful." There were tears in her eyes. "They just wouldn't part from one another, you see, and it was impossible to get any sane person to— Oh!"

Don started to laugh. Cathy stared at him and started to laugh, too.

"If we admit we're probably not completely sane, will you promise not to tell anyone else?" Don demanded.

"Never!" the sister swore, crossing herself.

Don looked at the kids.

"All of us?" David said yet again.

"All of you!" Cathy said.

"It's going to be Christmas with the Angels, guys, from here on out, okay?" He ruffled David's hair. "*All* of you."

Cathy began to laugh. The sister began to cry happily and hug the kids.

David said, "You mean *all* of all of us?"

"Absolutely all!"

The sirens were ceasing to shriek. The injured were being taken away.

One of the men from fire-rescue walked by them, shaking his head.

"Can you imagine? This *mess,* and not a single soul killed. It's a miracle!"

Don smiled. It was a miracle all right. A Christmas gift.

Long, long ago, there had been a gift to mankind.

A gift of love, the gift of life.

He and Cathy had received a very similar gift that night.

Life.

And love.

And both to be used to the fullest.

That darned car radio just kept playing and playing.

Christmas carols.

Don started to laugh again. His turn. He tilted back his head and shouted out a cry—to heaven.

He looked at Cathy. Smiled.

She shrieked.

He pounced. And they lay in the snow. Angels in the snow, he thought, and laughed and laughed . . .

Then kissed his Angel.

And wished her a merry, merry Christmas.